Celebrating 35 Years of
Penguin Random House India

Read more by Andaleeb Wajid

When She Went Away
Mirror, Mirror

Read more for young adults from Duckbill

Zen by Shabnam Minwalla
The Magicians of Madh by Aditi Krishnakumar
Miracles for the Maharaja by Aditi Krishnakumar
Murder in Melucha by Aditi Krishnakumar
The Lies We Tell by Himanjali Sankar
Talking of Muskaan by Himanjali Sankar
Zombiestan by Mainak Dhar
Jobless Clueless Reckless by Revathi Suresh
Facebook Phantom by Suzanne Sangi
The Right Kind of Dog by Adil Jussawalla
Shiva & the Rise of the Shadows by Kanika Dhillon
Daddy Come Lately by Rupa Gulab
Unbroken by Nandhika Nambi
Invisible People by Harsh Mander
When Morning Comes by Arushi Raina
Year of the Weeds by Siddhartha Sarma
Queen of Earth by Devika Rangachari
Queen of Ice by Devika Rangachari
Queen of Fire by Devika Rangachari

the henna start-up

ANDALEEB WAJID

duckbill

An imprint of Penguin Random House

DUCKBILL BOOKS

USA | Canada | UK | Ireland | Australia
New Zealand | India | South Africa | China | Singapore

Duckbill Books is part of the Penguin Random House group of companies
whose addresses can be found at global.penguinrandomhouse.com

Published by Penguin Random House India Pvt. Ltd
4th Floor, Capital Tower 1, MG Road,
Gurugram 122 002, Haryana, India

First published in Duckbill Books by
Penguin Random House India 2023

ISBN 9780143463689

Typeset in Book Antiqua by DiTech Publishing Services Pvt. Ltd

www.penguin.co.in

1

Ammi asks something and looks around at all of us.

No one answers.

I don't even hear her over the sound of Billie Eilish softly crooning in my ears. 'Wait 'til the world is mine.'

Ammi's looking at me expectantly, so I pull off my earphones and let the wires dangle around my neck.

'You asked me something?'

She nods. 'I asked you for today's gold rate.'

I groan and shoot a glance at Abbu, who's sitting on the other end of the sofa, sipping his tea. He doesn't have Billie Eilish in his ears, but he's so lost in the news that he hasn't heard her at all.

'Ask Abbu!' I tell her.

She shakes her head and indicates my phone. 'You check and tell me.'

'You check for yourself, no?' I tell her, balancing my plate on my lap precariously. 'I'm getting late for college.'

'I always end up somewhere else, Abir. Check and tell, no?' she says.

The slightly pleading tone in her voice does it for me. With a sigh, I pick up my phone, pause the song just as Billie's getting to the good part, and google for the day's gold rates. I show the phone to my mother whose eyebrows go up in worry, predictably.

'I don't know why you're so worried about gold rates,' I say.

Ammi doesn't even bother replying. 'Apparently, they're asking for eighty sovereigns these days,' she mutters. 'How are we going to arrange so much and then do it all over again?'

Ammi glances at Amal, my younger sister. I don't want to get into a shouting match with her before class. But why is it that when Ammi sees me and Amal, she sees only the 'responsibilities' that they have in getting us married? Why can't she see us for who we are?

'First of all, who's asking for eighty sovereigns?' I ask her and immediately wish I'd kept quiet.

Amal, who has been reading a book while eating her breakfast, looks at us. As usual, she has been lost in her own thoughts. 'What's going on?'

Ammi sighs again. 'You know. The boy's side.'

'Which boy's side?' I ask, alarmed.

'Any boy's side. Any potential bridegroom. Your future family.'

I grit my teeth at her words but decide that I can't rise to the bait. I will get late for college.

I finish eating quickly and take the plate to the kitchen to wash up.

Nani ambles out of her room and smiles at me. 'Leaving?'

I nod. I don't have time to chat with her. I know she will be disappointed. But I don't want to be paired with—ugh, never mind—*that* person for my chemistry practicals today. If I don't leave *right* now, I'll miss the bus to college, and everything will go downhill from there.

I hurry back to the living room, where everyone is eating, as we have been for a few months since Nida Phuppu's kids accidentally broke the dining table legs. Don't ask what they did to break the legs. It is true, though, that the legs had been a bit shaky for a long time. Abbu had been furious when he saw the damage, but he has yet to find the time or the money to get it fixed.

I wish we could just chuck the table out and buy a new one. But imagine saying that to Abbu. He'd look at me like I had two heads and three legs.

I don't have time to document the many ways in which my home can be made a lot less shabby. There's the peeling paint (the house was last painted when Nida Phuppu got married eight years ago). Then there's the rickety furniture. And of course, everything related to electronics is outdated, barring my precious laptop and our phones.

I fix my earphones in my ears again and wrap my head scarf so that they are concealed under it. Ammi looks at me and makes a 'tch' sound.

'How many times . . .' she begins.

'Ya, ya, I know. I won't listen when I'm on the road. *Come*, Amal!' I tug on my sister's shoulder. Her school and my college are in the same direction, so we travel together.

She stands up and brushes away stray roti crumbs from her uniform. She's wearing a sweater *and* leggings.

'How are you not feeling cold in December?' she asks. I'm wearing my regular shalwar kameez.

'No time to discuss why our body temperatures are different and why my metabolism is superior to yours. Just come!' I nearly roar at her.

This gets Abbu's attention. He looks up at us and nods and then goes back to his newspaper. Ammi will get busy preparing lunch once we all leave, but first she walks us to the door.

I push my feet into my sandals and wait impatiently while Amal ties up her shoelaces. How on earth did I get a sloth for a sister? She's so infuriating.

Ammi watches us with a sad smile on her face. I wish she'd stop making that face. But I've seen that expression for a very long time, and I know what it means.

You're getting so big so soon!

We'll have to start thinking about your marriage any time now.

All the relatives are asking.

Gold rates are just going to keep increasing.

'Bye Ammi! Khuda Hafiz.' I lean close and hug her suddenly. My mother can exasperate me, but she loves us, even if that love is tinged with unnecessary worry about what our future families will be like. I wish she'd appreciate the family we have now. Neither I nor Amal are going to be getting married any time soon. I'm seventeen and my sister is fourteen. Ammi needn't worry so much already. But she does.

Amal and I leave our house in the tiny gully behind Commercial Street and wave at Mahim Chacha, who is waiting in his auto. He waves back at us. We hurry into the auto. Chacha will drop us off at the bus stand where we'll get on our bus.

I mentally prepare for college. *I will not think of that person. I will not think of that person.*

I guess I am thinking of that person already, but I will stop. This minute.

Amal and I get on the bus. It's one of those rare days when both of us can manage a seat.

'Don't even think about it,' I tell Amal as she looks around to see if she can pull out her book.

She sighs. 'So unfair. You can listen to music and I can't read.'

'What can I do if my hobby is better suited for commuting than yours?' I tell her with a superior smile.

5

She sniffs, irritated. 'But I was at the end of a chapter, Api!'

'And it will wait. Read it in your lunch break,' I admonish her.

'You are not the boss of me,' she says, folding her arms across her chest.

'I am. The boss. Of you,' I enunciate with a grim smile. I *do* love bossing over her, a bit too much.

'I'll get back at you. Just wait,' she promises.

'It's for your eyes, Amu. You don't want to ruin them by reading on a bus! It's too shaky!'

'They're *my* eyes!'

'And you're going to be a big star some day. Doing whatever it is you want. Do you really want . . .'

'Oh, shut up and go back to listening to Harry Styles!' she snaps. We've had this argument before.

'Chee. I wasn't listening to Harry Styles,' I tell her, shuddering.

'Why? What's wrong with him?' she asks.

'Nothing.'

We don't talk after that. I press play on my phone, and in my ears, Billie screams, 'YOU SHOULD SEE ME IN A CROWN!'

2

PCMC 22 23
Wednesday

Keerthi 17:10

Gupta ws mean to evry1 2day. Any1 know why?

Luke 17:11

How wld we no? N wht dz it mattr?

Keerthi 17:12

We cld have bunkd chmstry practicls and gone off smwhere

Nina 17:13

As your class rep, I'm going to have to report you if you plan to mass bunk a class.

The Other Group
Wednesday

Luke 17:13

Keerthi! Y can't u keep your trap shut? In the clss grp spshly with that spuy Nina?

Karthik 17:14

With due respect, Keerthi, you kind of walked into that one!

Keerthi 17:15

Oh no. I jst sw. Dint realize.

Neeraja 17:16

Hahahaha, Keerthi, now she will lecture us tmrw.

17:16

Issok Keerthi. Happens.

Arsalan 17:16

What does your father ask when he wants to buy a beer? Can I have A-bir?

17:17

What your mother says when she looks at you and lovingly calls out to her Arse beta.

I put the phone face down. I'd done it again. But he really asked for it this time. He did.

Aargh. I hate him so much!

Luke is also often quite rude, especially in the class WhatsApp group, though he mostly ignores us in college. But somehow I don't feel the same kind of hatred for him.

'What happened?' Ammi asks as she places a plate of food in front of me.

I breathe out long and hard to let go of my irritation.

I will not carry my annoyance with Arsalan back home.

I repeat the mantra in my head, look up at her and smile. 'Nothing. The usual.'

'You study too hard,' Ammi says. 'See how hunched you've become?'

'Ammi, please. I'm fine,' I insist before she can get started on how my bad posture will hinder my chances of getting good proposals.

I look around our small home. I love this time of the day. It's just us women in the house, sipping tea and talking. Even Amal puts away her books until Abbu is back from his shop. Nida Phuppu and Samreen Khala complain about their respective mothers-in-law while Nani listens to them wide-eyed. Since my dadi passed away long ago, Ammi doesn't have a mother-in-law to complain about, and anyway, she never did.

Ammi loved Dadi like her own mother, and Nida Phuppu like her own sister, Samreen. So she wouldn't upset Nida Phuppu by talking trash about her mother.

When I was young, I used to think that after we left for school, Ammi had all the time in the world to herself to watch TV, read books or just enjoy life while we struggled with multiplication tables and fractions. But then I discovered that Ammi hardly ever had any time to herself. Especially since she started the henna business about five years ago.

Okay, so here's the thing. No one refers to it as a business because the word is too big and scary, but Ammi, along with Samreen Khala and Nida Phuppu, have been taking on commissions to do henna for a couple of years.

It's all through word of mouth. Someone who knows someone asks someone if they know anyone who can apply henna for weddings or functions, and it trickles back to Ammi, who is excellent at it. If she has time, she goes, and if not, she sends either of my aunts, if they're free.

I feel they charge a pittance. Abbu doesn't even know how much Ammi and the aunts get paid for this. I can't understand why.

'Why isn't *your* time and talent valuable enough to be paid for?' I asked her once.

'It's not that. I do this in my free time. I don't want him to think that he's unable to meet our expenses in any way,' she said, as if it were a perfectly understandable explanation.

The discussion today is about our dining table. Apparently, Ammi has saved enough money to fix it, but she can't because Abbu will want to know where she got the money.

I mutter, 'Just *tell* Abbu it's your money!'

'But he thinks all my money is his money. That it comes from him,' she says, shaking her head.

Nida Phuppu looks guilty because her children were responsible, after all, for breaking it, but she knows Abbu won't agree to taking money from her to fix it, because she's his younger sister. Then, her face brightens. 'Bhabhi, why don't you tell Bhaiya that you've been saving the money from the monthly expense money he gives you?'

Ammi shakes her head. 'That hardly covers all expenses any month. I always ask him for more before the end of the month.'

I share a look with Amal, my determination to be financially independent growing deeper with every conversation at home. The fact that my mother cannot use the money *she* earned to fix our dining table because it would hurt Abbu's ego is beyond my understanding. Okay, I *understand* it well enough, and I get where Ammi is coming from. But it seems like the height of irrationality to me.

And I am determined not to fall into the same pattern. Ammi thinks that once I finish college, I'm going to be sitting around at home, waiting to get married. I'll have to gear up for all the big confrontations coming up.

But now we have to think of fixing the dining table in a way that will not make Ammi feel guilty or Abbu suspicious. Ammi doesn't want to lie to Abbu. She also wants to make sure that he never learns anything unpalatable about what he can and cannot do for us. I am sure that after the initial ego problem, Abbu won't mind. But Ammi is adamant about this.

I'd rather not be bothered about whether this will hurt Abbu's ego. But one lesson I've learnt early on in life is that we have to choose our battles. This one's not worth fighting.

3

'**I**'m quite sure he likes you.'

I turn to Amal, a frown on my forehead. 'Who?'

'Sahil.'

I sit up in bed. 'What?'

Amal and I share the same queen-sized bed, and she sits up too.

'I mean it,' she whispers.

I want to tell her not to talk rubbish, but my sister isn't the sort to just make up things. Even though half the time her face is buried in a book, she's observant and very analytical.

Something hot claws up my throat. 'What makes you say that?'

Sahil is Samreen Khala's brother-in-law. He's in his first year of software engineering and is a couple of years older than I am.

He's also very cute.

Okay, cute might be the wrong word. Cute makes him seem like the needy kitten who's always mewling at our doorstep every evening.

Sahil is more than that. He's tall and has dimples and a proper chiselled jawline. But more than that, he has a very disarming smile. He likes to stop and chat with Ammi and Nani whenever he drops by to pick up Samreen Khala, as he did this evening. He doesn't chat with us because there's always some sort of protocol about talking to guys. Ammi wants Amal and me to go inside our room whenever he drops by, so we're not in his field of vision. But of course, we don't really listen.

Amal and I make some excuse or the other to come out and talk to Samreen Khala and pretend that we've only just noticed he's there too. That's what we did this evening as well.

Amal looks at me and shrugs. 'I don't know. It's just a feeling I get.'

Sighing, I fall back to my pillow. Amal and her feelings are useless. And I don't really want him to like me.

Here's the thing: from the time that Samreen Khala got married, which was about three years ago, Sahil has been one of the very very few young men that Amal and I have met. So it has kind of become a thing for Amal and me to joke about him and pretend to get excited.

When I was about Amal's age, I probably did have a tiny crush on Sahil. After all, he was pretty much the only young man that I saw up close. This had long faded, and I was determined that romance was not going to be part of my life now. But I still got a bit embarrassed at any mention of Sahil.

I am a science student, and while I love computers, I *do* understand biology. So while I don't fancy Sahil, yes, I like being around him and maybe even talking to him. I feel a little breathless and excited and happy. But what of it? I get breathless and excited and happy whenever we go to Wonderla too. Also, watching him get flustered in our presence is fun, and well, he's more than cute.

I don't have the time for boys. I need to get good marks in my exams, pass the competitive ones, and find myself a good college so I can become a top-notch software engineer. And then I need to get a job that will pay me enough to buy all the Lancôme moisturiser I want for myself and Amal and Ammi. Nani won't use anything other than Ponds cold cream, sadly.

'Okay, it's more than a feeling,' Amal admits, waiting to see if I will bite the bait.

I don't. It's been a tiring day that went off to an awful start because I'd been paired with Arsalan for chemistry practicals.

No. I will not think about him before I go to sleep. God forbid he appear in my dreams!

Amal is so quiet that I turn to her to see if she's fallen asleep. Her brow is furrowed, like she's thinking very hard.

I nudge her, and she blinks and looks at me.

'What happened?' I ask her.

'Nothing,' she says.

'Something happened at school?'

She shakes her head. 'No, why?'

'Just thought I'd ask,' I mumble as I shut my eyes.

'But you know what I think?'

I sigh and look at her again. If there's something in her mind, she will make sure I hear it, whether I want to or not.

'What?'

'I think you and Sahil would be *really* good together.'

'Amu, it's okay. I don't want all this jhamela, yaar. I've got all my life plans in place. I can't have anything messing all this up.'

Amal shakes her head regretfully.

'What?' I feel a little defensive.

'You're too analytical, you know?'

'So are you. And it's a good thing. More girls should be like us.'

'I'm not like you,' she says, a little dreamily.

I look up at the ceiling. 'You are, Amu. We're both sorted, and we know what we want. It's not marriage to some cute guy who happens to look at me for a few seconds longer than he should.'

'Who even talked of marriage?' she asks.

'It has to lead there, no?' I ask her.

She rolls her eyes. 'Fine. Be the grandmother you are. Don't come to me when you realize you're old and shrivelled at twenty and all the cute guys have been taken.'

I have a feeling she's right on some level. Maybe I am taking this a little too seriously. But I don't have time for all this nonsense.

Today has been really exhausting. Apart from the awful time in college, I had to try to figure out the situation with the dining table. There has to be a way to work this out, but thinking about it has given me a headache.

I fall into a listless dream, one involving a dining table, with Sahil and Arsalan both facing off sitting on *top* of it. I'm watching the two of them with my hands on my hips. Just as I yell and ask them what the hell they're doing, the dining table collapses and crashes to the floor.

I wake up, rubbing my eyes blearily. I might have to lobotomize myself if I want to make sure Arsalan doesn't creep into my brain.

4

Keerthi waves at me when I enter the classroom. I smile as I walk towards her and trip over a backpack that suddenly appears in front of me. My reflexes are quick, so I don't fall over, but I stumble a little.

Of course, it's the Arse.

I can see his stupid designer sneaker on the long leg that pushed the backpack in my way. His arms are folded across his chest as he eyes the ceiling very nonchalantly.

Of course, he knows I'm not buying it.

I've been taking the high road with him, trying not to get riled up, not letting him push my buttons — apart from occasionally losing my temper at him on the unofficial class WhatsApp group.

Pity, it's not his backpack, or I'd have just kicked it out of the way. Summoning all the indifference I can, I walk towards Keerthi.

She looks worried at my expression. 'What is it? You okay?'

'Of course.' I sit down on the bench and adjust my head scarf so I can get some air. My face is hot. I really need to splash it with cold water.

'I'm going to need your physics notes, okay?' she whispers as Mrs Kannan strides inside the classroom.

'Didn't you take photos of the notes last week?' I ask her, a little annoyed.

'Yeah, but I need the notes for this week, no?' she says plaintively.

'Why can't you write them like everyone else?' I whisper because Mrs Kannan is standing at the lectern and staring down at the noisy class.

'I lose track,' she whines.

'Do it during lunch time. I'm not missing my bus because of you again.'

She makes a face but nods. Then she bats her eyelashes and smiles. Huh?

It's not directed at me, of course. She's smiling at Arsalan, who, for some reason, has turned around from his seat and is staring at the two of us. He lifts an eyebrow, and there's a smirk on his face before he turns back around.

'How come he's sitting up front?' I ask Keerthi in a low voice.

She shrugs delicately. 'How am I supposed to know?' She smiles secretivly. This is why she doesn't take notes. The fool is probably dreaming about dancing on some Swiss slopes in a flimsy saree while Arsalan gazes at her with lovelorn eyes.

Arsalan happens to be annoyingly good-looking. There isn't a single reflective surface that he passes by without checking out his hair or his face. Conceited ass.

The whispers begin to die down, and Mrs Kannan starts her lecture. Everything else drowns out, barring her voice and the sound of my pen scratching on my notebook as I take notes furiously.

At the end of the period, Mrs Kannan adjusts her spectacles. She is also our class teacher and often takes the precious few minutes between classes to give us life gyan.

'The college wants to encourage young people like you to start taking your lives seriously. There is a campus incubation programme being planned. I want you all to consider applying for it. At the end of it, promising ideas will be selected for pitching before a jury. The people with the best ideas will receive mentorship and help from visiting consultants.'

'A jury?' Luke asks.

Mrs Kannan nods.

'Like *Shark Tank*?' he persists.

A buzz breaks out in the classroom.

Mrs Kannan looks aggrieved. 'Yes, something like that. This programme is being conducted by the college for undergraduates and postgraduates, but I see no reason why you shouldn't apply.'

Mrs Kannan leaves. As we wait for the next teacher, I put my books inside my bag and pull out the ones for the next class. Keerthi nudges me.

'What?'

'Look at them!' she whispers. A large number of people are talking excitedly around Arsalan and Luke's desks.

'So what?'

'You think they'll enter something for this incubator thingy?' she asks, her eyes wide with excitement.

'I have no idea.'

'I'm sure they will. They're always coming up with cool ideas.'

'Like *what*?' I ask her, unable to control the sarcasm in my tone. The day Arsalan comes up with a 'cool' idea, I might just change my name. No, wait. Why should I change *my* name? I'll change *his* name in my phone contact list.

'I don't know,' she says dreamily. 'Maybe he'll come up with an idea that no one else has thought of before. He can, you know.'

'Again, like what?'

Arsalan throws his head back and laughs. Then he carefully pushes a lock of hair back and shakes his head, as if to set the lock in place.

'Umm . . . I don't know. Maybe a delivery app for messages, but not on phones — those we write by hand.'

'We already have the postal system for that,' I tell her, patting her shoulder.

'Right,' she winces. Then she brightens up. 'Maybe he'll come up with an idea to . . . to . . . look at the sky and figure out if it will rain.'

I take a deep breath. 'What do you think the weather station does?'

'What do *I* know?' she pouts.

Arsalan looks in our direction, and we're both gazing at him. Aargh. I turn away quickly, but I still catch the smirk on his face.

Keerthi clasps her hands together. 'He smiled at me!' she says breathlessly.

I don't break the news to her that one day, I'm going to break those shiny white teeth of his, and then his smile will not look so good. And I don't look back in his direction.

5

When I go back home, Ammi has gone for a bridal henna appointment. Nani informs me that this is a big one. The dulhan lives in Benson Town, which is populated by the old moneyed types in Bangalore.

'How did they hear about Ammi?' I ask Nani.

'Through WhatsApp,' Nani says, with a gleam in her eyes. 'I got to know that they have a few more weddings in the family. If they like your mother's work today, they might call her again. It will be a lot of work, so your aunts will accompany her.'

'You know Ammi's back hurts when she does this for a long time,' I remind Nani.

She nods, some of the light going from her eyes. 'I forgot about that. I was just excited that this could be her big break.'

'But a big break to do what?' I ask her.

Nani shrugs. 'That's also there.'

'Has she gone alone?'

'Nida has gone with her.'

Nani had been somewhat of a rebel in her time. She didn't conform to the family regimentation and didn't expect her daughters to do so either. But she had been at a disadvantage because, even though she had been educated in school, going to college or working had been out of the question in the 1970s.

Nani's father thought that if she studied enough to teach her children and write letters to them, that was enough. But Nani used to hang around whenever the men in the family talked about business. Then she started helping Nana out with his work, offering such good solutions that he turned to her more and more.

She had wanted her daughters to study and work, and by the time they were of college-going age in the 2000s, it had not been that unusual. But Ammi hadn't gone to college. She had been doing II PUC when Abbu's rishta arrived. Nani hadn't wanted to get Ammi married so early, but the elders in Nana's family had insisted that it was perfectly all right to get an eighteen-year-old married to a twenty-five-year-old. I was born a year later, and Ammi's education was no one's priority after that—including hers.

This family history made me all the more determined to succeed. Of course, Ammi didn't feel she had missed out on anything. She would only tell me that Abbu had given her everything she needed. Which was true in its own way, but what was the harm in aiming higher? In asking for more out of life?

Yes, I'm ambitious. I don't believe that ambition is ugly or not suitable for girls.

'Nani, imagine what Ammi would have done if she'd finished college and got a job before getting married?' I muse as Nani watches me scarf down a slice of chocolate cake that Ammi has baked.

Amal looks at me thoughtfully. But she doesn't say anything.

Nani shrugs. 'She could have done amazing things. She is so talented and focussed. But Abir, it's important to remember that your mother is happy with whatever she has and whatever she has done.'

I don't think that's entirely true. Amal and I share a look, but we both stay quiet. I'm willing to let Nani believe what she wants.

Ammi comes back an hour later, a few minutes before Abbu is due to be back. Though Abbu knows that Ammi goes to do henna, Ammi likes to pretend that she has been home so that Abbu doesn't feel like she's neglecting housework. I wonder how Abbu would react if he knew how much money Ammi makes. Would he be mildly impressed? Or mildly threatened?

Ammi washes her face and makes sure Abbu's tea is ready. I want to see what would happen if Abbu's tea isn't ready on time *one* day. But we'll never know, will we?

I notice that something is different about her.

'Ammi, what happened?' I ask her as she finally sits down.

'What? Nothing,' she says.

Amal shakes her head. 'No, something is wrong, and you're not telling us.'

'Nothing is wrong,' Ammi laughs shakily.

'We'll just ask Nida Phuppu,' I tell her, reaching for my phone.

She tries to stop me, but Abbu enters, and she's distracted.

I take my phone to my room, and Amal follows.

Nida Phuppu answers on the third ring. 'What's up?'

'Did something happen today?' I ask her without any preamble.

'Bhabhi said something?' she asks sharply.

'No, she didn't. That's why I'm asking. What happened?'

Nida Phuppu sighs. 'The family we went to today asked us to do a full elbow-length henna design for the bride. And also ankles, feet and legs.'

Whoa. 'And?'

'We told them that it would cost 15k and they agreed. It took us *hours* to finish it!'

'And?' I ask, anger rising as I guess what happened.

'They paid us just half, Abir. Bhabhi was so upset. But you know how she is. She didn't want to fight or argue with them. She didn't want to make a scene.'

My blood is boiling now. 'You didn't say anything?'

Amal looks at me, worried.

'I tried to fight with them, but Bhabhi stopped me. She said we were getting late and insisted we go back home. My fingers are all cramped, Abir. We worked so hard and to not get paid for all that time and effort!'

'Can you give me the address?' I ask in a quiet voice.

'Why?' Nida Phuppu sounds worried.

'Just give it, please.'

'Don't do anything rash!' Phuppu warns.

'I won't,' I lie. And I note down the address.

After dinner, I see Ammi rubbing her hands with hand cream. I sit down with her and massage her joints. I feel terrible that she should go to so much trouble and not even get paid for her efforts.

Ammi didn't know that I knew what had happened. I tell her. She is not pleased with Nida Phuppu telling me.

'These things happen, Abir,' she says with a shrug.

No, they don't.

Abbu calls out to her, asking her to come to the terrace to see the sky. It was something my father liked to do. I used to get annoyed whenever he would call her up because she would leave whatever she was doing and go to him. Sometimes, I used to traipse along as well.

Now that I'm older, I understand that in a small house like ours, the terrace is the only place my parents can have a quiet conversation without one of us barging in. They can be people in their own right instead of our parents. They can even be romantic with each other, I guess. Gross.

Anyway, Abbu calls, and she answers that she is joining him. That is it.

She ruffles my hair as she goes. 'It's okay, Abir. These things happen. I'm used to such disappointments in life. Not everything can go our way, right?'

Her words of quiet acceptance make me even more determined to get even with this bride and her family.

I must look mad as I storm into our room because Amal looks at me with scared eyes. 'What are you going to do?'

'Decimate them,' I tell her firmly.

6

I have a feeling it's going to be a good day.

I arrived at college and discovered that Arsalan hadn't come. Class will be so much more stress-free.

It's a Saturday, so we have classes only for half the day. I call Ammi from college and say I am going to Commercial Street with Keerthi to do some shopping. Ammi is surprised and asks what I was planning to buy. I have to make up something on the spot. I say that Keerthi lived in a gated community and only went to malls for shopping, so she was dying to visit Commercial Street.

(This much is true. Keerthi moved to Bangalore a year ago and hasn't seen much of the city apart from the malls and the traffic.)

The truth is that we have no such plans.

The first hitch comes when I start to leave class. Keerthi stops me. 'I thought we were spending the afternoon together. Shopping?'

I frown at her.

She explains. 'Oh, I heard you talking to your mother. I thought it was so sweet of Abir to show me the other side of Bangalore.'

Oh. Oh god.

'Listen, I lied to my mother,' I tell her.

Her eyes widen. 'Why? You're off to meet someone?'

'Who?' I ask, baffled.

She nudges me playfully. 'A boyfriend. That's who!'

I sigh in exasperation. 'I don't have boyfriends, Keerthi. You'd know first. Listen, I . . .'

I look at her disappointed face, and I feel bad. Maybe we can go to Commercial Street after I've decimated the bride's family.

'So Keerthi, first we have a detour,' I tell her.

Her eyes widen. 'Ooh, is this where the boyfriend comes in?'

I slap my forehead. 'There is no boyfriend. I have something to do before we can go shopping. Is that okay?'

She shrugs. We walk towards the bus stop.

Keerthi stops me. 'Where are we going?'

'To the bus stop.'

'We can just take an Uber, can't we?' she says.

I shake my head. *No way am I spending any more money than is necessary on this.* She thankfully doesn't offer to pay for the Uber.

We wait for the bus, talking about this and that. I discover that Keerthi has no five-year plan, let alone a ten-year plan. This shouldn't surprise me. But since I have been planning what I want to accomplish month by month, year by year, since I was about twelve, it makes me wonder how others go through each day without knowing that they're one step closer to their goal.

When we sit down in the bus, she turns to me. 'So *you* have a plan then?'

I nod, but I don't tell her that I have a plan for the next twenty years of my life in five-year segments. She won't laugh at me, but she might let it slip in front of others, and they won't hesitate to mock me.

She tells me about this reality TV show *Love is Blind* that she's watching. I don't think I would spend even ten minutes on it, so I can't imagine how she binge-watched an entire season.

'So it's just like an arranged marriage but for white people?' I ask her incredulously.

'I mean, it's not like . . .' she trails off.

'And people are watching this?'

'Yeah. I guess,' she says, looking thoughtful.

The whole concept of marriage is strange to me. Why can't people just let girls be? Why the heck do they start talking about marriage the moment a girl reaches a certain age? Why would any girl voluntarily want to get married if she did not have to?

My extended family has been talking about my marriage for ages now, and I'm just seventeen. How does it fulfil them really?

I know I have a long battle ahead of me because once I finish my degree, my uncles and aunties are going to start hounding my parents to get me married. Can I see myself as the dutiful bahu of a family, taking care of them, being selfless and everything?

Nope.

Not now. Not ever, I guess. My parents are going to be shocked when I tell them that my future plans include getting a master's degree, preferably in a different city, so I don't have to deal with this crap any longer.

When we get off the bus, Keerthi looks around with fascination. 'Which part of Bangalore is this?'

'The old, moneyed part,' I tell her. 'The part you know — the gated communities and condominiums and malls — isn't really Bangalore. That's just all new.'

'Oh, Abir, promise me you'll show it to me!' she says. 'And I can't wait to go to Commercial Street now.'

I feel a bit uneasy that I might have oversold it. 'It's just a couple of streets where you get clothes, shoes and stuff.'

Her eyes light up. 'Shopping! Yay, thank god I carried my add-on card today!'

This isn't the time to dwell on how different our lives are. I have to focus on showing this rich family that I mean business. But I'm not sure what Keerthi will say when she learns that my mother applies henna for brides.

I decide not to tell her. In fact, I decide to make her wait in a park so I can go do my thing on my own. I feel better already.

As we near my destination, I spot a park. 'Listen, can you wait for me there?'

'Why?'

'I have to talk to someone. It's a little private. I'll come back and we can go to Commercial Street,' I tell her.

She doesn't ask me any questions but heads towards a bench in the park, pulling out her phone.

I hitch my abaya up a little so it doesn't trail the road and walk determinedly to my destination.

7

It's hard not to gape at the mansion before me. I double check the address to see that I'm at the right house, though I am pretty sure because it is lit up with what seems like a billion lights. They're barely visible because it's bright sunlight now, but it must be very bright at night.

These jerks don't even bother to switch off the lights during the day, but they can't pay my mother what she worked hard for?

I stomp towards the gate, fuelled by righteous indignation.

A security guard stops me and asks who I am.

'I have come to apply mehendi for the dulhan.'

He frowns. 'Didn't they come yesterday?'

I nod. 'Yes, I came to finish the job today.'

He lets me inside.

There is a huge lawn, around which there is a large sweep of driveway with many fancy cars lined up. Through the large open glass doors and floor-to-ceiling windows, I can see many bejewelled people milling around.

I feel self-conscious. With my plain grey abaya, my backpack and my headscarf, I don't look like a girl who should be going in through the front door. I remind myself of my mother's aching fingers. I leave my footwear outside and walk in purposefully.

No one notices me. I can see other people—workers, servants—walking carefully around the periphery of the giant hallway with its huge, sweeping flight of stairs, trying not to get in the way.

There is a woman who I think is the woman of the house. She has that air of authority. She's wearing a champagne silk saree, her throat glittering with a diamond-encrusted gold necklace. She looks elegant, though her makeup is a bit over the top.

I walk up to her as she is issuing instructions to three assistants. 'Are you the bride's mother?'

She turns around and eyes me. 'Who are you? How did you get inside here?'

'I'm Shahana Maqsood's daughter, and I walked inside.'

She looks a little irritated. 'Who's Shahana Maqsood?'

I'm not surprised that she doesn't know Ammi's name. 'The henna artist who applied the henna for your daughter last evening.'

There is sudden understanding and a certain craftiness in her eyes. She straightens her back and looks down at me. 'So?'

'I came for the balance payment, aunty!' I tell her with a smile. I just know being called aunty by me will annoy her.

'We cleared the account yesterday. There is no balance payment,' she says imperiously and way too loudly.

A few curious glances are cast at us.

She notices, so she comes closer. I get a whiff of a spicy perfume that makes me want to sneeze. 'Stop making a scene!' she says angrily but more softly.

'Oh, I haven't even started yet,' I tell her. I pull out my phone and aim the camera at her.

'What are you doing?' she asks shrilly. She tries to grab my phone, looking enraged. The bad makeup looks like splotches of red on her face as I step back.

'I'm doing an Instagram Live for your daughter's wedding!' I tell her brightly.

'You will do no such thing,' she says, trying to grab my phone again.

'Oh, the world needs to know how you transact business,' I tell her, my finger hovering over the live button. I don't want to really broadcast to the world. If I did, word would travel back to Ammi. And not in a good way.

'You little chit. How dare you!' she snarls.

'Just like you dared to not pay my mother for her work!'

'I will blacklist your mother!' she shouts.

'Once people start seeing this live, then they'll know what sort of person you are. Imagine your daughter's in-laws seeing this, *aunty*?'

These are apparently the magic words. Her bravado fades and she makes a really ugly face.

'What's happening there?' a man calls out.

I think it's her husband. I turn to him, aiming the camera at his face.

'Oh hi, uncle! I'm just here for our balance payment!' I tell him. He frowns.

'Shut up,' the woman says. She grabs my arm, her nails like claws, and drags me to a room. 'I'll pay you, you cheap little extorting piece of shit.'

The words hurt me more than her claws. But this is not the time to be hurt. I am here to get justice for Ammi.

She unlocks a cupboard and pulls out a wad of notes. She counts them out rapidly and hands a bunch to me. I take them and check the amount.

'What about the mental harassment?' I ask her.

'The *what*?'

'What my mother had to endure when you refused to pay her the money.'

Her face turns red. 'You . . .' She notices the phone in my hand and with a disgusted noise, peels off a few more notes and hands them to me.

'Thank you.'

I take the notes and put away my phone. She looks like she wants to hit me.

'Thank you. It was good doing business with you.' I smile sweetly, though there is a loud buzzing in my ears.

I walk out of the room and head to the front door. My eyes briefly meet those of a pretty girl walking down the stairs—she is clearly the bride.

As I am slipping my feet into my shoes, the man who had earlier called out comes up to me.

'Did you get the balance payment?' He has kind eyes and a warm smile on his face.

I don't want to like him, but I do. 'I did, uncle.'

As I walk down the driveway, a car pulls up. It looks familiar. The door opens, and Arsalan steps out.

Only—it's Arsalan in a black pathani with gold embroidery. He looks nothing like the swaggering fool from college.

My eyes widen in shock. I don't want him to see me here. He's probably a guest at the wedding, because isn't that how it is? All the rich people know each other from breathing in the same rarefied air.

I put my head down and walk quickly. I can't understand my actions. I should have stood my ground. I have nothing to be ashamed of. But the woman's behaviour combined with the kindness in the man's eyes and Arsalan in a pathani has thrown me.

I reach the gate and make my escape.

8

Keerthi and I have a good time on Commercial Street. It's really different shopping with someone who has the money to spend and who doesn't think twice before buying anything.

And she doesn't bargain!

Her eyes grow wide when I knock off at least two hundred bucks from the jootis that the man in one of the by-lanes is trying to sell her.

He looks at me up and down and glares. 'What are you doing with my customers?'

'What do you mean?' I ask. We speak in rapid-fire Dakhani, and Keerthi doesn't seem to follow, even though we're still speaking Urdu.

'I know you. You live here, nearby. Why are you spoiling my sales?' he asks aggressively as he hands Keerthi's jootis to her with an ingratiating smile.

'What's it to you?' I ask hotly.

Sensing some drama brewing, Keerthi drags me away and suggests we go to the nearest Starbucks to drink a frappé and cool down. I burst out laughing.

'Surely there must be a Starbucks nearby?' she says, looking around. 'I mean, this place is filled with shoppers.'

I shrug. 'Yeah, there is. There's one not too far in Kamaraj Road, but let's go to this other place.' I lead her down one of the busy inner bylanes. My house is not too far from here.

'There are more shops?' she asks, eyes wide.

I nod. 'This is Ibrahim Saheb Street. A lot of people shop here and not in the main Commercial Street.'

'Why?'

'It's cheaper?' We always shop at Silver Plaza or the adjacent Diamond Plaza for dress materials and never bother going into Fazal; there's a huge price difference.

I lead her into Sagar Chaat House. As we walk past the huge tawa where the potatoes for the pav bhaji are bubbling away, we are assailed by all kinds of sounds and smells. The sizzle of the sandwich maker as a fat pat of butter is dropped on it. The tak-tak at the pav bhaji counter as the man hits the tawa with the long-handled spatula to bring the masala to the centre. The scraping of the benches as people push them behind, ever so slightly, to sit down.

Keerthi smiles widely. 'This is so, um, cute!'

One of the tables has just been freed up, and we quickly grab it and drop her packages on one end of the bench.

'Whew, thank god,' I mutter.

Keerthi is looking around wide-eyed. 'This place is so small!'

I nod. 'Yes, there's an upstairs also, but those stairs are ridiculous.' She turns around to where I am pointing and shudders. Just climbing those stairs is painful, and I'm not even middle-aged with bad knees. Also, the waiters take forever to bring food.

We order a plate of masala puri and pani puri each, to be followed by hot chocolate fudge.

'That's all this costs?'

'Don't put nazar on it now,' I tell her crisply as I take the menu from her and hand it to the waiter. He has been seeing me since Amal and I were toddlers and would come here with Ammi or Samreen Khala and munch on sev while they gossiped and ate spicier stuff.

'This is so quaint,' she says as she looks around again.

I feel the tiniest burst of irritation. I couldn't stand Keerthi when I first met her. I thought she was a spoilt airhead. She's still all those things, but she's also very sweet and kind and never thinks badly about anyone, and somehow, we became friends.

She straightens up. 'I'm sorry. I know, I know. My worldview is limited, and I'm privileged, and I acknowledge that privilege. But Abir, your worldview is limited too, isn't it? You should come over to my side and see it sometime!'

My jaw works silently as I consider her words.

Her side. I just walked out of a house that was easily on her side than mine. I'd been humiliated by a rich woman, whose saree probably cost six months' rent for us, because I asked for my rightful dues.

'What's there to learn about your side, Keerthi?' I ask as the waiter brings the plates of masala puri. Steam wafts up from it. Keerthi looks puzzled.

'This is a Bengaluru take on chaat. It's not what you're used to, but you might just enjoy it,' I tell her, a little annoyed that she won't be answering my question after all. Simply because she has no answers, I'm sure.

But to my surprise, Keerthi looks up. 'You're right. My side is a bubble, and I've lived in it all my life. I never considered half the things that you tell me about.'

I try not to think about all the things I've had to tell her over the past few months because there are too many. And instead, I think about someone else, from *her* side. My super-brainy brain had to remind me suddenly how Arsalan looked in the black pathani.

So, here's the thing — I like to think I'm invincible. I like to think I can take on the world with the power of my convictions and the strength of my ambitions. But my one weakness (one of many that I will probably figure out later, I'm sure) is men wearing black pathanis.

I grit my teeth as I push my spoon into the masala puri and swirl it around to cool it down a bit.

I will *not* be brought down by a black pathani.

9

'I'll drop you wherever you need to go.'

'Actually, I live nearby. I can walk to my house from here,' I tell Keerthi.

'You live *here*?' Before I can assume she's being classist, her eyes widen. 'Wow. What fun! Imagine just walking out of your house and down to Commercial Street!'

I grin at her. 'Yeah, that's there.'

There's an awkward silence. I realize too late that she's waiting for me to invite her to my house. I'm not ashamed of my house. Okay, well, I *am* a bit embarrassed about it, certainly.

My house redefines clutter. It's everywhere. There is something on top of something on top of something in every inch of the house. Keerthi's house and her room—I've seen photos on Instagram—are all lacquered cabinets and glossy marble floors and elegant empty spaces. I haven't visited yet, though she keeps inviting me.

'So, I'll see you on Monday in college then,' I tell her brightly.

She walks away, waving a cheery goodbye.

I feel terrible. I want to explain to her why I don't want to invite her home, but that would be even lamer, wouldn't it?

I walk back home thoughtfully, trying to arrange the events of the day in my head. I know I'm going to be in trouble once Ammi knows I got her money. Thoughts of Champagne Saree are enough to bring me back to my vendetta-ish best. I straighten my back.

At home, Amal is busy doing some school project on the floor near the sofa. Her back is hunched, and her hair is falling over her books. This is why we need to fix that dining table. We *will* get it fixed. When Abbu asks, I'll tell him that it's my money. If Ammi won't lie, I don't mind doing it myself.

And thank goodness I didn't bring Keerthi home to this. Amal sprawled on the floor, Nani cracking walnuts on the sofa, dropping the sharp bits of shells everywhere that she will recruit us to collect (otherwise they're going to poke our butts when we sit down), and Ammi peeling smelly garlic for the adrak-lahsun paste that's the holy grail of all cooking. Nani's TV serial is on at high volume because that's how she likes it. We've all got used to it by now. Keerthi would have been horrified, and I would have been mortified.

'Where were you all this while?' Ammi asks.

'I told you I was going shopping with Keerthi.'

Amal looks up and sniffs. 'I smell chocolate. But not the good kind. You went to Sagar and had hot chocolate fudge?'

'Yeah. With Keerthi,' I add quickly. The hot chocolate fudge there is not as good as the chaats.

I look at the the ageing wall clock above the TV. There's still time for Abbu to come. Better get this over with now.

'Ammi, I know you'll get angry, but I had to do it,' I tell her as I pull out the money and hand it to her.

Nani fumbles for the remote and puts the TV on mute because her inner radar tells her that this drama is going to be more entertaining. *Okay, that's mean.* Maybe Nani just wants all of us to hear each other clearly without shouting. But the sudden silence in the living room is unnerving.

'What's this?' Ammi asks, her hands freezing in the middle of smashing the garlic cloves.

'The money you were owed for your job yesterday.'

'Abir! You went there?' Ammi asks, her voice rising in shock and anger.

I'm not a child. I'm not five anymore. I won't fear her anger.

I quail inside. Then I recall Champagne Saree and stand straight.

'Ammi, you can't let such people run rough-shod over you!'

I love my mother madly, and I often give her snarky replies. But I am a bit scared of her icy-rage face. Like now.

Amal is looking at us with wide eyes. If only my sister had more courage than a rabbit, she would have stood up for me, like I'd stand up for her *any* day. 'What did you do?'

'I went to her and told her that she should pay the balance amount, and she did.'

'Abir!' Ammi says in a warning tone.

'Okay, I pretended to do an Instagram Live to name and shame them. It worked! Why are you angry?'

'Because what izzat will we have?' she asks.

I shake my head. 'We never had any izzat where they were concerned. So why does that . . .'

Ammi stands up. 'Abir, sometimes I really wish you were a boy. Then you can say such rubbish and get away with it. I walked away from there because I didn't want to make a scene. I walked away because I need more business, and I won't if that woman bad-mouths me everywhere.'

Champagne Saree had said she would blacklist Ammi. I decide not to tell Ammi this.

'And think of the consequences sometimes at least, will you? What if someone who's connected to that family learns of this, and we get a rishta for you from someone who knows them and . . .'

Oh god, this again? 'Ammi, that's still far off. I won't be getting married for another ten years at least!' I interrupt her impatiently.

This shocks my mother into silence. 'You mean you won't marry until you're twenty-seven?' she whispers after a few moments.

I shrug. 'Twenty-seven isn't old.'

Ammi lets out a shaky breath. 'Abir, you have some very strange ideas about the world but I'm not going to get into that. You'll learn about it yourself very soon. Tell me what happened when you said that to her. About the Instagram thing.'

I shrug again. 'She was rude, but she gave me the money and even a little extra.'

Ammi shrinks back in horror. '*Extra*?' she asks, like I've stolen the money.

'For all the mental trouble she put you through. It's legit money, Ammi,' I try to tell her.

Ammi is shaking her head. 'Keep it.' Her tone is so incandescent with rage that I'm shocked. I'm not the golden girl at home, but Ammi is usually mild-mannered.

'But . . .'

'I don't want it. Keep all the money. Do whatever you want with it. Buy all those creams you keep looking at on your laptop.' She walks away regally.

I feel dumbfounded and hollow. Deep inside, I want my parents to acknowledge my strength and resolve. The realization that I so badly want their approval does no good to my self-esteem. I thought I'd crossed this stage long ago.

I stare at the money in my hands. I know that repairing the dining table with it is not going to do me any favours. So what the hell do I do with it? And how do I make Ammi not mad at me anymore?

10

It's the weekend. Usually, I really wait for these because I don't have to spend a major part of my day being a study-focused lunatic.

But this weekend is really weird and awkward. Since Ammi doesn't want to yell at me in front of Abbu, she just gives me cold looks and avoids talking to me unless absolutely necessary.

It's the dreaded silent treatment.

By Sunday mid-morning, I'm crawling out of my skin in agitation and the unfairness of her anger.

'Okay, so I might have come on a bit strong with that woman,' I tell Amal in a heated whisper when she comes inside to keep the folded clothes in her wardrobe. 'But if I hadn't shown spine, that woman would have picked me up like a cockroach and flung me away!'

Amal shrugs helplessly. She hates being stuck between me and Ammi. She's the mollifying sort who diffuses confrontations, so I suppose she also thinks I'm wrong. When I say this to her, she shakes her head.

'No, not at all. Actually, I can't even imagine having the guts to do what you did. But you have to understand Ammi's point of view too, right? She's mild-mannered and . . .'

'Except when it comes to me!' I interrupt her.

'She feels this makes her look like unprofessional — someone who sends her daughter to collect money.'

I guess Ammi has a point. But if she doesn't stand up for herself, I have to. Otherwise, people will walk all over her. Like Champagne Saree did. 'I'm convinced I didn't do anything wrong, so if she's expecting an apology . . .'

Amal rolls her eyes but doesn't say anything.

'Listen, what if we ask a third party about what I did?' I suggest.

'Who?' she asks, narrowing her eyes. 'Nida Phuppu?'

'Let's ask Samreen Khala. She is not a pushover, and she will tell us like it is.'

Amal nods. 'Okay.'

I call Samreen Khala. She sounds harried when she answers after a few rings.

'I want to ask you something,' I say.

'Abir, can it wait?' she asks and then calls out to someone to stir the onions before they turn black. I realize that she's probably cooking the big family lunch they have every Sunday at her place.

Amal and I look at each other. 'Okay sure.'

She senses the change in my tone. 'Hmm, listen, I have an idea. Why don't the two of you come for lunch today? We can talk while I'm cooking.'

I shake my head and realize that she can't see me. 'No, no, we don't want to impose.'

'Rubbish. I'll speak to Apa and tell her to send the two of you,' she says crisply.

I groan out aloud. 'Ammi is going to hate me even more. She won't like us going there for lunch, right?'

Amal shrugs. 'Who knows what Ammi will say? Her moods are so unpredictable. She might think it's a good idea to be rid of us for the afternoon.'

We hear Ammi's distinctive ringtone and then the murmur of voices. We look at each other.

'Amal!' Ammi calls out.

Amal jumps as if she has been caught with her hand in the proverbial cookie jar and rushes out. My sister would make a terrible spy. 'Yes Ammi!'

I listen as Ammi informs her that the two of us have been invited to Samreen Khala's for lunch.

'Wear something nice and go. And try not to step out in front of any non-mahram men,' Ammi says.

Why should we bother dressing up at all? I don't want to argue the point. Amal runs inside, eyes wide.

'What?'

'Let's get ready. You wear that bottle-green shalwar kurta you wore for Eid,' she says.

I frown. 'No! That's too grand for this . . .'

'I assure you, it's not grand. Women wear those sorts of clothes at home all the time.'

'But why?' I ask as I rifle through my wardrobe.

'That's what they do,' she says as she hunts through hers.

'No, I meant, why do you want me to wear that outfit now?'

'For someone who's so smart, you can be such a thickhead, Api,' she mutters.

'Hey!'

'We're going to Samreen Khala's house,' she says.

'I know.'

'Sahil will be there too, right?' she reminds me in a loud whisper.

I roll my eyes. 'So?'

'So, wouldn't it be nice if you were looking pretty?'

'Ammi told us not to step out in front of any non-mahram men,' I remind her.

'I know . . . but he might just accidentally walk in on us when we're talking to Samreen Khala. It's better to be dressed nicely, right?'

I wonder if my sister only playacts being absorbed in her own world. Maybe she knows fully well what's going on in the world, sometimes even more than me.

11

Samreen Khala lives in Fraser Town, which is not too far away. It's still a headache to get an auto.

When the tenth auto has asked us for Rs 150, I turn to Amal. 'Let's just walk there.'

'No!' she says, shaking her head. 'No way, Api. I don't know if you care about your clothes, but I'm not about to ruin mine!'

'How will walking to Samreen Khala's ruin our clothes?'

'Sweat stains!' Amal hisses. We're already sweating under our abayas and head scarves.

Fine. 'If we don't get an auto in the next five minutes, we're going back home.'

She looks dismayed. I did want to get out of the house and away from Ammi's chilly glare. Also, I'm hoping that Samreen Khala will tell us that Ammi is in the wrong and I am right. Not that it would do me much good because I don't think Ammi will ever consider herself wrong.

Amal shuts her eyes and mutters something under her breath. It sounds like a dua. To my extreme surprise, the next auto agrees to take us to Samreen Khala's without asking us which part of Fraser Town we want to go to.

Although Uber and Ola autos do work, it's not easy to get them here, for some reason. Maybe they realize that this is the OG auto ilaaka and they're not going to get any app-based rides here.

I know Ammi is not pleased that we're going, but she doesn't want to be rude to Samreen Khala. Amal is holding on to the box of mithai that we were instructed to buy from Bhagatrams.

We're both quiet.

What if Samreen Khala too thinks that I was an idiot who should have minded my own business? I feel a bit silly now. In college, I strut around like such a know-it-all, reeling off facts and figures and slaying annoying boys who try to intimidate me.

And then, of course, a flash of Arsalan in the black pathani appears, and I shut my eyes. I hate this. I almost wish that I see him in college tomorrow, because I know he'll be neck deep in some stupid shit and that will immediately replace this image I have of him now.

Why did he have to look so good in it? Aargh.

Samreen Khala opens the door before we can ring the doorbell. She looks as harried as she sounded but she eyes us dubiously. 'Why are you two wearing makeup?'

'What? What makeup?' I sputter.

OF COURSE, WE'RE WEARING MAKEUP.

When there's a good chance of us bumping into Sahil, we're not going to look like our skin isn't this dewy all the time, are we?

The house is filled with the fragrance of delicious food, and my stomach gurgles involuntarily. Ammi's weekly special meals are on Friday, when she makes biryani or khushka khurma, or sutriyan or on the very rare occasions, khichda. But Samreen Khala's family convenes on Sundays for their family meal.

'Take off your abayas in my room. Then, come help me a bit, okay? We can talk there,' she says, walking away towards the kitchen.

Amal looks down at the pale yellow shalwar kurta she's wearing and sighs. 'I think you were right.'

'I always am, but right in what way?' I ask her as I tidy my hair under my head scarf in front of Samreen Khala's dresser.

'We are a bit overdressed for Sunday lunch,' she says ruefully.

'It's okay, Amu. The clothes won't get ruined if we do a bit of kitchen work.'

We head to the kitchen. The house has two levels. The ground floor has two bedrooms, a hall and a kitchen, while the first floor has two bedrooms. We don't bump into Sahil on the way. I know he lives upstairs.

Samreen Khala's mother-in-law lives in the other downstairs bedroom. Though she seems like a harmless old lady, I've heard many odd tales about her from

Samreen Khala, especially how she likes to manipulate her sons all the time. Besides Samreen Khala's husband, Sadiq Uncle and Sahil, she has an older daughter, Arjumand, who lives across the town.

This kitchen is nothing like the one in our house. Ours is a long strip where people can stand comfortably in a row. This one is a large square with counters and cabinets and even a small kitchen island with a few chairs. It is a buzz of activity. Something is bubbling away on the stove, which Samreen Khala is stirring. It smells amazing. A maid is dicing vegetables at one of the counters.

Samreen Khala's mother-in-law is at the island, slicing almonds. She looks at both of us, her smile not quite reaching her eyes. We try to act as if we're demure girls, and butter wouldn't melt in our mouths. I don't want Samreen Khala to hear taunts about how her sister hasn't brought up her children properly and that maybe it's a good thing she hasn't had children yet.

Just like every other family I know, this one too looks normal on the outside but is a teeming mass of insecurities inside. Samreen Khala has been married for only three years, but she hasn't had a baby yet, which has led everyone in the family and everyone who knows the family, even peripherally, to recommend all sorts of treatments to her.

The mother-in-law looks really old. I mean, how did she have Sahil at whatever age it was she had him when she looks like she could be knocked down by a feather? I shudder. *Not knocked down, but knocked up*, I think with a mental groan. *He must have been an accidental baby.*

Never mind. I'm not going to think about *his* parents' sex life, for the love of god. Mine are bad enough with all the gooey eyes they make at each other when they think no one's looking.

But now that my mind has switched tracks, I can't help but wonder if his father met his end while he was, um, *with* his mother. If *she's* already so old, he must have been so much older.

Urgh.

We won't be able to talk freely with the old lady sitting here, I think. But of course, Samreen Khala has a way out.

'What should we help with?' Amal asks uncertainly.

Samreen Khala beckons. 'Here, take this cup of tea. It's for Amma,' she says. Then she turns to her mother-in-law. 'Amma, you should sit outside in the living room and have tea. There's a nice programme on TV. He will be joining you there once he returns from the market.'

Ah, so that's where Sadiq Uncle is, I think.

'He and Sahil have both gone out, but they'll be back soon,' she tells us and turns away. And I am glad because I'm quite sure she would have caught the googly eyes that Amal makes at me.

Thankfully, her mother-in-law allows herself to be led outside by Amal, whom she starts asking all the intrusive questions extended family always asks. The maid also leaves the kitchen, leaving just Samreen Khala and me.

Samreen Khala nods to the plate of almonds and indicates that I should continue slicing them. 'Now tell me,' she says. 'What's going on?'

12

When I finish telling her everything, Samreen Khala looks thoughtful. 'So what do you want me to do?'

I make a face. 'Tell me who's right here!'

Samreen Khala puts her hands on her hips. 'Do you think it will make any difference where your mother is concerned?' she asks wryly.

Amal comes back, looking queasy.

'What happened?' I ask her.

'Nothing. Nothing,' she says with a weak smile. I'm sure the old lady must have battered her with questions, from our wedding plans to whether my parents have thought of having more children in the hope of having a son. She sits down beside me and looks at Samreen Khala, hopefully. 'Well?'

I shrug, annoyed. 'I don't know. She's not saying anything.'

'I didn't *not* say anything,' Samreen Khala avers. 'It's just that no matter what I think, it's not easy to get your mother to change her mind. You know that, right? It's a fact.'

'Well, at least I'll have moral bragging rights,' I mutter as I nearly slice off my finger while trying to chop the stupid almonds.

Sighing, Samreen Khala switches off the stove and sits down. 'Look, what you did was courageous but also very stupid.' As I open my mouth to protest, she shakes her head. 'Listen first. No one from that family will call your mother or us again. And they might badmouth us to their acquaintances. Bangalore is a hive of gossip, you know that, right? But you fought for the rightful fees, and that's good. Just don't expect the world to applaud you for doing what's right.'

I digest her words. 'You mean, I should do what *looks* right, but it may not always *be* right.'

Samreen Khala smiles. 'I really, really hope that the world doesn't douse this fire, Abir,' she says. '*How* did you get to be this way? It's something I always wonder.'

I don't know how to respond but I'm disappointed. I'd thought she would rail against the unfairness of Ammi's treatment of me.

'You're scared of Ammi too,' I tell her flatly. 'That's why you're giving this diplomatic non-answer.'

'I'm not!' she protests. 'But Abir, not everyone is like you. People quail at the thought of asking for what's rightfully theirs. Maybe you going ahead and doing this made your mother feel inadequate. Did you ever think of that?'

I pass the almonds to Amal, who starts pulverising them.

Samreen Khala has a point, but right now, I just want to do something that will ensure that my mother will never be humiliated this way again.

'I've been thinking,' I begin, and Amal groans.

'What?' I turn to her, irritated.

'That sentence always backfires and most often on me!'

I turn back to face Samreen Khala. 'I've been thinking that we should figure out a way to streamline the henna business. Make sure that clients pay a booking fee through UPI maybe. Or ideally, even pay the full amount in advance according to a rate card. But I'm not sure how to make it happen.'

'A website?'

Sahil is standing at the door. *How long has he been there?*

Amal nudges my leg, and I want to tell her that yes, of course I know he's there.

'A website?' Samreen Khala asks, looking doubtful.

Sahil walks inside, pulls up a chair and sits down opposite us. 'A website sounds like a good solution,' he says.

A little nervously, I nod. 'Yes, but how?'

Sahil shrugs. 'I can develop it.'

Samreen Khala's face lights up. 'Really?' she asks. 'How would it work?'

'There are lots of website builders that we can use, but I can code it too, so we don't have to rely on an external CMS.'

Amal and I share a look. 'I don't know if Ammi will agree,' I tell him.

He frowns. 'But why won't aunty agree? This way, you can easily get bookings through the website, and we can configure a payment gateway as well.'

I don't know why I haven't jumped on the idea yet, because it is a good idea. I wish I'd thought of it. Somehow, my competitiveness will not abate, even when a cute guy comes up with a good idea.

I look at Samreen Khala for help. 'You know how Ammi is,' I tell her. 'What do you think she will say?'

'I think Apa will agree,' Samreen Khala says. 'I'll talk to her. I'll tell her that Sahil will build the website for us.'

'But won't it cost money?' I ask.

Sahil nods. 'We'll need money to get the domain and the hosting. But after that, it's fairly simple.'

'But will people even use the website?' I ask sceptically. 'How will they know we have a website?'

'We can send links to people through WhatsApp and social media. Once people start using the website, it will completely change the way you guys run this,' Sahil explains earnestly.

He's right. It will completely change the way the henna business runs. But I'm still irked that I didn't think of it.

13

'**A**ctivist?'

I frown at Ammi as I walk inside our house, followed by Amal, who's holding on to the tiffin carrier that Samreen Khala had insisted we take with us, filled to the brim with the Chinese fried rice that we'd had for lunch.

Ammi is talking to someone on the phone and squinting. Who is she talking to?

'Okay. Okay, sure. No, it's not like that, but . . .'

Ammi squints again.

'Okay. Thank you. Really. Okay, sure,' Ammi ends the call and looks perplexed.

'What happened?' Amal asks.

Ammi has forgotten that she's not talking to me. 'That was the bride from the other day.'

My stomach sinks. Champagne Saree's daughter?

'What did she want?' I ask sullenly.

'She said that she didn't know my daughter was an activist, and she was sorry that there was a mix-up with the payments.'

My eyebrows go so far up into my hairline that I don't know if I can bring them back down.

'And?' Amal prompts Ammi.

'And that's it. She said she was sorry and that she hopes our services will be available for future weddings in her family, especially in her sasural.' She narrows her eyes at me. 'So what you did made you an activist?'

I shake my head. 'No, I just asked for our due. But if they want to think that, let them.'

Ammi seems a little mollified by my answer, or maybe it was the weird apology from the bride that has soothed her ruffled feathers. 'How was lunch?'

Amal brings forth the tiffin carrier. 'Samreen Khala sent some for you and Abbu,' she says. 'It's not leftovers.'

Ammi wrinkles her nose briefly. But then she smiles.

Sadiq Uncle's family is richer than us, so there's some complicated up-and-down system I don't even try to understand. Sometimes, Abbu gets angry when he sees us get food from there, but other times he's okay.

Ammi surprises me. 'So, you still have that money?'

I want to ask 'What money?', but I don't. 'No, I spent it all on retinol and serums and moisturisers.'

Ammi pales. 'What?'

'Of course, I have the money.' If I were a nicer person, I would just give it to her, but I want some payback for the silent treatment yesterday.

'Can I have it?' Ammi asks. 'So we can get that dining table fixed.'

I blink in surprise. 'Really? You're doing it?' I ask her, swallowing thickly. 'What made you change your mind? What about what Abbu will say?'

Ammi sighs. 'Well, if my daughter can be an activist, the least I can do is stand up to my husband and tell him I can get things done too. And we don't have to always depend on his money.'

My jaw hits the floor. 'Really?'

'No, not really. But it's time to get that table fixed. I'll tell your abbu I saved the money over a few months,' she says briskly.

It's a start. At least, things are getting done. I get the money and hand it to her. She still looks at it a little distastefully. 'Thanks.'

I'm smart, so I don't say anything.

As Amal and I go to bed, feeling happier, I suddenly remember that I haven't told Ammi about the website. I worry a little about the money for the domain and hosting. But first, I need to convince Ammi that this is a good idea.

Tomorrow, I have college. Something inside me tightens. I realize with some chagrin that it is anticipation because I'll see Arsalan.

He's not going to show up in the black pathani, I tell myself. *He'll be in his usual torn jeans, tight t-shirts that show off his biceps, and that annoying smirk that makes him look like a proper idiot. And my heart will not skip a beat. Pucca.*

Amal murmurs sleepily.

'What?'

'I don't understand why that bride called Ammi today of all days,' she says.

'Why?'

'She would have been in the middle of the wedding. Why did she think of doing this? Where did she find the time?'

That's true. I hadn't thought of that. 'Who knows?' I mutter. My brain can't take any more drama.

14

Arsalan is absent. My chest stops being so tight when I don't see him lounging at the college entrance. And when I don't see him in the first class, my body relaxes.

'How was your weekend?' Keerthi asks, bumping my shoulder amicably when we sit together in physics class.

'We spent all of Saturday together,' I remind her.

She makes a long-suffering face. 'Fine. How was your Sunday?'

'It was actually very interesting,' I tell her with a smile. I suddenly feel like sharing more with her, even though I know that it is very likely that she might squeal.

'So,' I begin, and she directs her gaze at me.

'So?' she asks.

Am I really going to do this?

'There's this guy I know,' I begin, feeling a bit foolish, 'and he had a really good idea . . .'

Keerthi's mouth drops open so dramatically, it's almost comical. 'Details!' she gasps. 'Give me details.'

'No!' I say. 'It's not like that. He just had . . .'

She interrupts me again. 'What happened?'

'Nothing *like that* happened,' I tell her as if I'm talking down a terrified five-year-old who accidentally got on a roller coaster and had her guts whipped around mercilessly.

I give the extremely abridged version—Sahil is my aunt's brother-in-law, he's a couple of years older than me, blah blah blah . . . .

'So, wait. If you get married to this guy, your aunt's mother-in-law would be *your* mother-in-law?' she asks.

Shit. But also, double shit. I laugh shakily. 'Please. Let's not go there. Sahil is cute and everything but this story is not about romance. Also, I'm not going to get married for the next ten years at least.' *Why had I uncapped this bottle with Keerthi?*

'Okay, so what were you guys talking about?' she asks.

I'm proud of my mother. But at the same time, I'm aware that it makes us look like we need money from every quarter. So I am a bit hesitant as I tell her about the henna business and how I'm thinking about starting a website.

Keerthi's eyes widen once more. 'Your mother does mehendi for brides?'

I nod. I pull out my phone surreptitiously and show her some of Ammi's designs.

She's awed. 'This is amazing. And the website sounds like a great idea.'

Our physics teacher, Ms Vishwanathan, walks in.

Arsalan trails in behind her. He's dressed almost respectably for a change. No torn jeans or tight t-shirt. My mind immediately presents the image of how he'd looked on Saturday. *No, we're not going there,* I tell my mind firmly. *No pathani.*

Ms Vishwanathan gives him a sardonic look. 'Found the time to come to college, Mr Khan?' she asks him.

'Unfortunately, yes, Ms Vishwanathan,' he says with such a genuine smile that the hard-nosed teacher actually smiles back at him.

I'm gripping my pen far more tightly than I should. This is what I hate about him. He can be a snivelling charmer with the teachers and a complete jerk with us. And we all know which are his true colours.

He lopes up the steps gracefully, and his gaze finds mine. To my horror, he winks. It's so quick that I don't know if it really happened. Not until Keerthi clutches my hand.

'Arsalan winked at me!' she whispers.

Behind us, I can hear a couple more girls.

'He winked at me!'

'No, he winked at me!'

If I ever had to write an essay about all the things I hate about Arsalan, I would find it hard to decide what would go on top.

His smile? His lazy glance? His shiny white teeth, that I have the utmost urge to break? His hair? His strong, corded biceps? His . . .

I straighten my back. I had no idea that I had such a huge list of things to hate about him.

I'd strap myself to the railway tracks before I ever admitted such a thing. But the truth is, he had winked at *me*.

15

I refuse to be one of those confused girls who moon over some unachievable guy. So I wipe out all thoughts of Arsalan's wink and focus on my physics notes.

When class finishes and some students leave to attend other classes, Arsalan and Luke walk to the second bench at the bottom of the class and seem to be in serious discussion. Our classroom is cavernous and designed like an auditorium, with the desks and benches arranged on broad steps that go right up to the back.

Keerthi wants to casually bump into them and ask what's going on. And she wants me to come with her.

'I give you full permission to get my teeth extracted without anaesthesia before I do something like that,' I mutter.

She gives me a chagrined look. 'Why, Abir?'

Maybe it's the guileless look on her face or my guilt at not having invited her home on Saturday, or something else but I shrug. 'Fine. Let's bump into them casually.' I will just stand behind her, looking disinterested, because I don't want Arsalan to think that I'm wary of him or avoiding him.

It was a stupid, meaningless wink.

Delighted, Keerthi drags me down the steps. When she said casually bump, she had meant bump *literally*. She slips and goes sprawling forward. Since her hand is still clutching mine, I go down too, propelled forward by momentum.

Luke sees us and nimbly moves out of the way. He extends his arm to catch Keerthi, and she lets go of my hand.

Arsalan's head turns as my feet skid down the steps and his eyes widen.

I have a brief moment of panic that I'm going to barrel into all of them, and we'll all be in a heap on the floor.

Arsalan pushes Luke and Keerthi out of the way and extends both arms.

Like Shahrukh Khan.

The horror in my face triggers a smile on his as I slide right into his arms. Both of us stagger back a little from the impact, but Arsalan doesn't back further down the steps.

Whistles and claps ring in the classroom. I try to disentangle myself from his arms. His stupid, steely, muscly arms. He lets go of me immediately. I am breathless from the contact. My mouth is dry, and I know my face is aflame from all the attention in the classroom. Totally, the wrong kind of attention.

I straighten.

'Are you okay?' Arsalan asks, his voice a whisper that does funny things to my insides. 'Or shall I get you . . . a beer?'

I move away from him, glad of this reminder that he's nothing more than an 'Arse'. I don't make the quip. I don't want to hang around.

I think Keerthi can see that on my face. She winces. 'I'm such a klutz!' she says, rubbing her arm where Luke probably gripped her too hard.

'Actually, that's what we're working on,' Luke says. 'Something to help klutzy people. We're actually working on a prototype of sorts to pitch to those startup investors.'

Arsalan looks away from me and joins Luke on the bottom step. 'Yeah,' he says. 'Though Luke is being kind, I have been quite . . . busy, so it's actually his idea, and he is doing all the work. I barely know anything.'

Despite the embarrassing moments I've just experienced, I'm intrigued.

Keerthi looks excited. 'Oh, I'd love to listen in to you guys talk,' she says, her eyes growing round in unnecessary hero worship.

Luke looks pleased. 'If we leave now, we can bunk the next hour.'

'We're not bunking any classes,' I tell him loftily, wondering if I can just find a place to sit here, so I have a valid reason for coming down the steps. But the front seats are already full with the girls who are a tightly knit clique.

'Can you move out of the way?' Nina asks irritably. 'You're blocking the path.'

Arsalan steps to one side and down, and I try to move back up.

Keerthi puts out her hand and grabs mine. 'Come, no,' she pleads.

I *have* bunked classes before. And I'm also curious. What did Luke mean about the pitch?

A slow sort of idea begins to grow in my head.

I can guess it would be expensive to make an app. *But what if I can pitch that idea before this jury? Wouldn't that be better than a website?* I get the feeling that this idea is gold. And it has nothing to do with me wanting to be more accomplished than Sahil.

And wouldn't it help to hang around these two to find out more? To see what needs to be done.

'Okay.'

Everyone is surprised.

Arsalan puts his hand on his chest for dramatic effect. 'This calls for a celebration,' he says.

'No beer jokes,' I tell him, lifting my head a little arrogantly. He smiles, and for once, I *don't* feel like breaking his teeth.

'I promise. On my very fine arse,' he says, patting said body part. Keerthi giggles.

The classroom has that hushed atmosphere that builds just before a teacher walks in.

'Hurry!' I tell them.

We leave quickly, just as the next teacher is rounding the corridor.

Keerthi is trying hard not to giggle, but she's looking very pleased, probably at the thought of spending the next hour with Arsalan.

'Where to?' I ask, looking around and hoping we're not spotted by any of the faculty.

'We have a spot in the college,' Arsalan says.

'Gross.' The word leaves my mouth before I can stop myself.

'Why?' he quirks his brow.

'I don't want to know about your make-out spots,' I tell him. 'I mean, you and Luke look good together, but it's a bit TMI for me.' It's my default reaction to try and push his buttons.

That's when Arsalan truly surprises me. 'Whoa, whoa, whoa. Luke and I don't need a make-out spot to kiss, okay?' he says. He swivels Luke around, places his hands on both sides of Luke's face and plants a firm kiss on his lips. 'See?'

Keerthi and I don't quite know how to react.

'And for the record, Ms Abir,' he adds in a low voice, turning his head to look at me. 'Luke and I are just friends, and neither of us swings the other way, *and* there was nothing gross about that kiss.'

16

Luke playfully shoves Arsalan. 'Dude, you don't have to worry about your reputation. *I* do,' he says.

Arsalan rolls his eyes. 'It's not like there's anyone here, and what's the worst that can happen?'

Why doesn't he have to worry about his reputation? I don't have time to think about it because they're already walking away. Keerthi and I hurry to catch up.

'I can't believe it,' Keerthi whispers. 'Of all the people he could have kissed in this college, he chose Luke.' She looks so agitated that I feel bad for her.

My mind is tracking through a hundred different things because it doesn't want to focus on one particular detail—the outer layer of my dislike of him seems to have disappeared in the last fifteen minutes. Actually, that is not true. The second layer. The outer layer of dislike had most definitely dissolved on Saturday afternoon.

Ten minutes later, we're sitting on a bench in a remote part of the college. I'm not surprised; I've never come across this space before. It's secluded, hidden among trees and leafy bushes, and far from the main gates or any of the buildings. There's something a little forbidden about it.

'Relax,' Arsalan says when he sees my expression. 'You look like you just passed by the garbage truck.' He's sprawled on the other bench, lounging like a nawab.

I bite down my urge to give him a nasty comeback.

Luke is walking around, explaining the concept to us, his eyes alight. 'I'm sure that as girls, you would have come across anti-skid pads and things like that to stick on the base of your shoes so they don't slip when you're walking.'

'I'm not sure why you needed to mention "as girls" because it's useful to everyone,' Keerthi says.

Luke frowns, but Arsalan sits up. 'Hey, listen to what she's saying,' he tells Luke. Keerthi's face flushes with pleasure. 'They're like our mock jury. And we have to be prepared for anything that the jury asks us.'

Luke goes on. 'Fine, *everyone* finds those anti-skid pads useful, right? But what if we're able to find a way to predict and stop you from slipping and skidding or whatever klutzy thing you end up doing?'

I cock my head. 'You do realize that this isn't science fiction? You're going to have to figure out how to predict this. How would you? You can't just throw ideas randomly and expect the jury members to believe they might work.'

'Patience, patience, Abir,' Arsalan says as Luke's face flushes.

No one in their right minds would believe that Arsalan and Luke are pitching their idea, pretending our opinion matters. I try to work up my indignation, but it's apparently hibernating somewhere.

Arsalan clears his throat and looks at me. It feels like it's just the two of us here in this remote corner of the college garden. If I were wearing one of those heart-rate-measuring watches, my heart rate would have been at least 130.

'Let the man talk,' he says.

Luke continues, 'So, we want to pitch an idea for a wearable device that can calculate how susceptible klutzy people are to a fall or a possible object they can bump into and warn them instantaneously.'

Huh?

'It's not that far off in the future. I'm sure someone somewhere already has the idea for it, and they're working on it,' he continues.

Keerthi looks quite dazzled. 'Is that even possible?'

'Sure,' Luke replies. 'It has to be AI-based, and we have to figure out how to actually make it happen.'

'AI?' Keerthi asks, frowning. 'Artificial Intelligence?' Her expression clears up, and she looks even more euphoric.

'Looks like Abir is not impressed,' Arsalan says.

'Again, do you realize that your pitch has to be doable? And not a flight of fancy?' I ask.

'Flight of fancy,' Arsalan says, rubbing his jaw with his thumb and forefinger. I notice the light sprinkling of stubble on it. This sudden, acute awareness is disturbing.

'Abir, you just solved a big problem for us,' he says.

'She did?' Luke asks, confused.

Arsalan nods. 'That's what we're going to call the app. Flight of Fancy.'

'Do either of you even know robotics or anything to do with AI?' I ask, irritated for some reason.

'Not really. But we can always figure out something,' Arsalan says confidently.

'So how do you plan to make the prototype?' I ask.

'That we'll do a dummy sort of thing to make it look believable at the pitch level,' Luke says.

For a few moments, I have nothing to say, so I just stare at the two of them. 'You're joking right?'

Keerthi looks at me. 'Why? It's a fantastic idea, no, Abir? I'd most certainly buy that device and wear it if it would stop me from being such a klutz.'

I sit up straight.

'It's a great idea, Arsalan,' I tell him. His face lights up in a way that is strangely heartwarming. But I push away the thought briskly. 'However, you have to show some sort of real science behind it. How are you going to predict that people are likely to fall? Are there any specific parameters you are going to measure? Are there any indications at all that one can measure which show people are prone to falling? Otherwise, this won't just be a "Flight of Fancy".' I make air quotes.

He frowns. 'Then?'

'It will be *khayaali* pulao, and I'm pretty sure the jury isn't interested in eating it,' I tell him as I get up and dust my clothes.

17

'**B**oys,' I mutter to myself as I walk away.

How presumptuous and superficial they could be!
I was part dismayed that they were going to make fools
of themselves before the jury and part eager to see it
happen. How could they think that just pitching any
random idea that came to their mind would work?

Keerthi follows me reluctantly.

'Hey, I don't want to miss the next class. You can
stay there and be their mock jury if you want,' I tell her.

She looks miffed. 'Why do you hate them so much?'

Behind her, I can see Luke and Arsalan having a
heated argument.

'I don't hate them,' I shrug. 'They're not that
important.'

Keerthi looks at me shrewdly. 'It's like reverse
snobbery, I guess.'

I look at her, surprised, as we make our way to the main college building. There's still some time before the next class. We start walking towards the canteen where we can hopefully get some filter coffee.

'Reverse snobbery?'

'Yeah. You think highly of yourself, and you have good enough reason for that, I guess.'

I'm a little annoyed, but I let her keep talking.

'And you look down on others who you think are of a higher social standing than yours or are rich, irrespective of whether they're intelligent or not,' she tells me.

We walk inside the canteen in silence. I'm not sure I can process Keerthi's words without getting angry. I've looked down on rich people all my life. Since school, rich girls have had their snooty noses in the air. They've given me so many condescending looks and been really mean about where I come from.

Keerthi looks a little dismayed when she realizes that I'm angry. 'I didn't want to upset you, Abir,' she says.

'I'm not upset.' I am beginning to acknowledge that she may be right, and that is unsettling.

'But you're angry?'

I open my mouth, but I am not sure what I want to say. 'When did this become about me?' I ask her finally.

'I've known you for nearly a year now, and we've spent so much time together. I've learnt a lot from you, but I've also noticed how you behave around a few people.'

My back stiffens. For some reason, Keerthi is determined to drop truth bombs today.

'I'm surprised you became friends with me. But be honest, okay? If I hadn't pushed and pushed, you'd probably be thinking the worst of me too, right?'

This much is true. Keerthi wormed her way into my life and became my friend without me realizing it.

'Let me get us coffee,' I tell her, by way of reply.

'Get me a samosa too,' Keerthi says.

I go to the counter to order, glad that Keerthi has never felt the need to be magnanimous in the canteen, by offering to pay every time. In fact, half the time we're here, I'm the one who pays. It's always made me feel good about myself, even though I might be panicking at how quickly my pocket money is disappearing.

I turn around to look at my friend. She's not the airhead she comes across as. She's shrewd and street smart, and so what if she's mooning over Arsalan? Half the class is, anyway.

I bring back the coffee and snacks to the table. 'Okay, you're right, but only to an extent,' I tell her.

Her face lights up. 'This moment needs to be documented, Abir!' she says, taking out her phone and snapping a photo of me.

I roll my eyes. 'For what?'

'This is a historical moment. The great Abir Maqsood just admitted that someone else is right! And that someone else is me!' she says in a grand voice. I realize that it wasn't a photo but a video that she's posting on Instagram.

I pick up the coffee and blow on top to cool it a little. Keerthi's expression changes suddenly and dramatically.

'What happened?' I ask her, sitting up.

She blows out a breath and looks back at her phone. 'Abir, I . . . um . . .'

'What?'

'Someone has taken a video of you falling into Arsalan's arms and they've posted it on Insta as a reel,' she says.

Please, please, no. I've always stayed off the social media radar. This is the last thing I need. If my parents ever found out, they'd be so mad. Abbu wanted me to attend a girls-only college, but I insisted on coming here because this college was so much better.

'Show me.'

Keerthi taps on the screen and hands her phone to me. I take it with shaky hands. The reel plays out. It was posted just half an hour ago, and it's already got a thousand likes.

No. No. Nooooo.

Whoever took the video—in this moment of stress, I don't recognise the name on the account—has slowed it down and added an old song 'Suraj Hua Maddham' as the soundtrack. It looks cheesy and ridiculous as I fall in slow motion towards Arsalan, who holds out his arms to me.

I'm glad that my face isn't visible. I had no idea someone had taken a photo, let alone a video of the moment. But then, the scene cuts to another angle, and in this, my face can be seen as I hold on to Arsalan's arms, and it looks like I'm gazing into his eyes lovingly.

'I think I'm going to throw up.'

'The coffee is that bad?'

I whip my head to see that Arsalan and Luke are right behind us. My face flames. I can't be here. I'm embarrassed and angry and humiliated.

'I have to go,' I tell Keerthi.

I walk away.

I'm going home.

18

My house is quiet at this time of the day. Nani is sitting on the sofa, dozing, her head drooping forward. I can hear sizzling sounds from the kitchen, so Ammi must be making lunch. Amal is still in school. Abbu is in his shop.

As I walk into the living room, Ammi comes out. She frowns when she sees me back home so early from college.

'Everything okay?' she asks.

'Yes,' I tell her without meeting her gaze. I'm terrible when it comes to lying to her. 'I have cramps.'

'But it's too early for your period,' Ammi remarks. *Who asked her to memorise our cycles,* I think irritably.

'It's not to do with that. I think I ate something that didn't agree with me,' I tell her.

'Like what?' she asks, frowning again.

'I don't know.' I walk past her to my bedroom.

All the way back home, I hadn't thought about the disaster that unfolded because I was sure I wouldn't be able to control my reactions. Now I lie on the bed and give myself permission to think about it.

I'm tired. This day has been strange. I hate that Instagram reel. I hate being in the spotlight for such silly reasons. I'm so annoyed at myself. I should have looked around to see if someone was taking a photo, let alone a video. I should have thought of all the possibilities when the classroom rang with whistles and claps. But all I could think about was . . .

Not going there.

Not going there.

I am not going to think about how it felt to clutch Arsalan's arms.

I hate him, I hate him, I hate him.

The litany in my head doesn't feel like it normally does. As if they are just words, and I don't really mean it.

Ammi pushes the door open and comes inside.

'Are you okay, Abir?' she asks, sitting down by my side and pushing the hair away from my face. 'Are you feeling feverish?'

I shake my head. I hate lying to her, but I can't tell her the truth either. My parents would not be okay with that Instagram reel. Ammi would be horrified at how my face and name are out there in the world for all the wrong reasons (I agree with her on that), and that I'm in the arms of some boy.

Oh god. And it had to be Arsalan?

I know Ammi will believe me when I tell her that it was an accident. But that will not lessen her anger. It might just make her rethink her decision of allowing me to attend a co-ed college. Who knows? My parents might pluck me out of college and make me do a correspondence course.

No.

I can't let that happen. I have to find out who posted that reel. I should have done that instead of coming home like a fool. I should have dragged that person over the coals and made them delete it. Why did I run away from college?

I know the answer.

It's because I didn't want to face Arsalan. I can well imagine the mocking look on his face when he sees that reel. Oh god, he's going to tease me about it for a long, long time, isn't he? He'll stop the beer jokes, and he'll hum 'Suraj Hua Maddham' whenever he sees me.

I try to keep my face blank.

'What's going on?' Ammi asks.

I think of the many English sitcoms that Amal and I watch, unable to believe the way parents are portrayed in them. Our parents can't be our friends, no matter how much easier that would make our lives. I think they would be horrified, and we'd be embarrassed. But a part of me wishes that we didn't have this distance between us. That we could connect at a level where I could tell her all that happened today.

'I think you're stressing too much about the exams,' she says.

I shake my head. 'No, it's not that.' Then, to distract her, I tell her about the idea for the website and how an app would be much better.

'Wait, a website? An app?' she asks, her eyes widening.

I nod as I sit up.

'For the henna customers?'

I nod again.

'But why?' she asks.

'If we set up the app, then customers can book appointments on it and pay up beforehand,' I explain.

She looks at me disbelievingly. 'Who will pay up *before*?'

'They will, Ammi. That way, no one can try to get away by not paying you for your work.'

'Abir, that's not going to happen,' Ammi says with a sad laugh.

'Why not?' I ask her stubbornly. 'Look, people pay upfront for services on Urban Company, right? They pay upfront for tasks to be done on Dunzo. So why not for henna?'

Ammi chuckles. 'Arrey. Those are essential services. Henna is not!'

'Ammi, what's the harm in trying?'

'But how will you do it? Do you know how to build websites or apps?' she asks.

'I do, but not perfectly yet. And anyway, Sahil said he would help.' The words slip out.

'Sahil?' Ammi asks, another frown marring her brow.

I nod uneasily. 'Yesterday, when we were talking about this with Samreen Khala, he came up with the website plan. But Ammi, I think an app would be so much better.'

'Where's the money going to come for all this?' she asks.

The thought that has been forming in my head all morning has solidified. 'There's a campus incubation programme in college, and we can pitch our idea before a jury. If they like it, they might help us with the investment and other stuff too. Who knows?' I shrug.

Ammi looks troubled. 'I don't know, Abir.'

'Why? You don't have to do anything. I'll work on a mock-up of the app with Sahil and . . .'

She draws in a breath. 'I don't think it's a good idea for an unmarried girl like you to be around a young man like him.'

My jaw works. I'm *unmarried*. He's merely *young*.

'Amal will be with me,' I mutter.

'Oh, so *two* unmarried girls around a young man then?' Ammi says tartly.

'Ammi, please. Don't make this a big deal. We'll be in front of you whenever we do this. We'll work on it here, outside in our living room.' I should have confirmed with Sahil first, but I don't think he'll mind.

Ammi's lips purse. 'And what will you tell your abbu?'

I rub my forehead in agitation. 'That's your job.'

'What? Why?'

'You need to own up to the fact that the henna thing isn't something you do as timepass. It's your *business*.'

Ammi's throat works a little, but she says nothing. She gets up. At the door, she turns around.

'Okay, Abir. Okay. Do this. Let's see what happens. But remember that this is all based on some jury liking your work. And that might not even happen.'

'Don't jinx us before we even get started,' I mutter.

Nodding, Ammi leaves. I'm glad she hasn't pushed, asking why I came back early.

My phone pings. I look at it reluctantly. It's a message from Keerthi.

I tap the screen to read her message.

It's gone. The video is gone.

19

The words don't make any sense to me. I saw the video on her phone, and the likes were going up before our eyes. How could it have disappeared?

I call up Keerthi cautiously, my heart racing. If she's still in college, she won't answer because theoretically, none of us are supposed to carry our phones with us.

But she answers immediately. 'Hey! Where did you disappear?'

I remember then that I didn't tell her where I was going. 'I came home.'

'Oh. But why? You just got up and left and anyway . . .'

'So that video isn't there?'

'No, it's gone,' she says firmly.

'But how?'

'How else do you think? Arsalan was so angry when he saw that video,' she says in a hushed voice.

'He went back to class and called out the people who posted the video.'

What?

Keerthi goes on. 'Yeah. He was mad. Rishi had taken the video and posted it. So Arsalan made him delete it. And then . . .'

My heart goes flip-flop in my chest. Why would he care?

'He went around the class and made sure whoever else had taken photos or videos deleted them from their phones.'

I don't know how to process this.

'Isn't he such a gentleman? I shouldn't have been surprised to think that he cared that much about your reputation and all that, Abir,' she says warmly.

Ah right. The penny drops.

'Keerthi, it's not my reputation, but his,' I tell her. This whole thing is embarrassing though, and I really hope she doesn't ask me to explain further.

'What do you mean?'

Outside, I can hear the door open and Amal's voice. She's back from school and she'll come inside any moment.

For some reason, the idea that Arsalan got that video taken down twists something inside. It makes me uncomfortable and even a little angry. And that's bizarre because I should be glad the video is no longer there.

'He doesn't want to be associated with someone like me,' I explain to Keerthi.

'Abir, that's not true,' Keerthi retorts.

'Listen, I know the sort of family he comes from.' Champagne Saree comes to mind immediately. Arsalan must belong to a similar family — rich, uncaring and extremely classist.

'And this isn't because I'm a reverse snob,' I tell her quickly before she can accuse me of that. 'He's most certainly not the sort to want to be connected to someone like me, especially in something like that video.'

Amal walks inside and looks surprised to see me in bed. I want to hang up because discussing this has made me feel very angsty.

But Keerthi keeps talking. 'No, I don't think so, Abir. He was quite angry about how people could have posted that video without your consent.'

'Listen, we'll talk tomorrow in college,' I tell her.

'You should thank him!' she says. I end the call without saying goodbye.

Thank him?

Despite whatever rosy ideas Keerthi has about Arsalan, I know enough about people like him. They care a lot about their reputation and the image they present. He may not have gone around and got the video taken down if it had been someone like Keerthi. They belong to the same class, economically and socially. They would have both laughed it off. Maybe that would have eventually led them to start dating each other.

The thought is acidic. Given how Keerthi has been trying to get Arsalan to notice her, maybe soon enough she and Arsalan will finally start going out. And then what? Then I'll lose my best friend to a boyfriend who would take up all her time, and she wouldn't have any left for me.

I drop the phone on the bed beside me as Amal starts pulling out clothes for a shower. I should have showered too, but I'm just so tired.

'Why are you home so early today?' she asks.

'I wasn't feeling too well,' I tell her. I can't tell Amal about the video.

My sister is far too perceptive. She shakes her head and sits down at the foot of the bed. 'No, something else happened. You're lying.'

I glare at her. 'Why would I be lying? Can't a person be sick?'

'When you're really sick, I know how you behave,' she says.

'What? How do I behave?'

'You act like the world is ending, and you're ending with it. You're perfectly fine,' she says, inspecting me from head to toe critically. 'But something else is up. Come on. Tell me all about it.'

I try the same distraction technique that I'd done with my mother and tell her about how we should work on an app instead of a website.

Her eyes widen. 'That's brilliant, Api! And what did Ammi say?'

'You know Ammi. She was worried about unmarried girls like us working with Sahil,' I tell her.

'So, I told her that we'll work here in our living room under her nose.'

She does a face-palm. 'You idiot.'

'I had to think fast!' I protest.

'But the app is a cool idea. Although, what sort of competition are you up against? What if you don't make the cut?' Amal asks.

'Let's not think that far ahead. Let's focus on what we can do.' The sort of competition I am up against could be fearsome. Not everyone will come up with silly pitches like Arsalan and Luke.

The thought of Arsalan makes me suddenly remember everything that happened in college today. If ever I do want to decode his actions today, I can't. And while I am tempted for a moment, I can't talk about him with Amal because . . . because I know she will read more into it. She'll jump to the silly conclusion that I, Abir Maqsood, flayer of annoying boys and slayer of mansplaining idiots, have succumbed to the charms of Arsalan Khan.

No.

If I don't speak out loud about it, it never happened.

'Why do I feel like there's something more you aren't telling me?' Amal says, getting up from the bed.

'You just have an overactive imagination. Go bathe. You stink,' I tell her, knowing that this will divert her.

With a glower, she bends down and removes her socks, balls them up and throws them in my direction.

'Yuck! Yuck!' I yell.

20

Abbu looks at the dining table and then at Ammi, who gazes resolutely at the TV, pretending that nothing is out of the ordinary.

Today, Ammi got the dining table fixed. When I had come home earlier, I'd been too distressed to notice. But when I stepped out of my room after Asr namaz for tea, I had seen it and marvelled. And now it is Abbu's turn.

'How much did it cost?' Abbu asks, scratching the back of his head.

'Surprisingly, not too much,' Ammi replies. Her nose is pink. It's a tell but not everyone knows about it since Ammi hardly ever lies.

But Abbu knows and he frowns at her. 'I asked how *much*, Shahana.'

Ammi glances at me almost helplessly. I pull out my phone and tap open one of the home service apps I had downloaded. I had been looking at several such apps all afternoon, making notes about what we should include and what we should be careful about, especially things like ease of use, the user interface and a clear rate card. I needed to do something to take my mind off the events of this morning.

'Abbu, we called these guys. It cost us . . .' I look down at the screen, trying to calculate how much it would have cost to fix a dining table, and then I look back at him. 'Around ₹650.'

He frowns, and Ammi gives me an exasperated look.

'That can't be right,' he says, walking close towards me to take my phone. *Uh oh.*

'Yes, see, they don't charge too much,' I tell him, backing away.

'Where are you going?' he asks, eyes narrowed.

'I have an important project to work on. I have to get started,' I tell him and walk back to my room.

'Abir!' Abbu calls out.

'I'll come out after half an hour, Abbu!' I call out.

Shit. I must have made things worse. I chew my lower lip anxiously and then peep outside. I can hear them talking softly. I really hope Ammi doesn't sell me out by telling him the truth *now*. I quickly make my way up to the terrace.

I hardly ever come here because there's no time. Once I'm back from college, I usually have assignments to finish and record books to complete and now that I missed out on half a day, I will have to catch up on that as well. But for a moment, I need to breathe.

I spot other people on their terraces, pulling dried clothes from washing lines and picking up dried chillies from spread-out cloths. I place my palms on the warm, gritty parapet wall.

The activity on the other terraces reduces as the sky turns darker.

It's that time between Asr and Maghrib when the world seems to slow down its constant motion, when everyone takes a pause, for maybe just an instant, before they pick up energy again and carry on.

It feels different to be out here at this time. A slight wind blows, bringing in various scents, including that of freshly baked biscuits from a nearby bakery. My stomach rumbles with hunger.

I know that it's time I stopped procrastinating and called Sahil. Without knowing what exactly I'll say, I call his number.

'Hello,' he answers, sounding surprised. We've never spoken on the phone before.

'Hi.'

'Abir? What's up?'

'So, um, I wanted to thank you,' I start off feebly. I stand straight. In the distant sky, through the polluted atmosphere, I can see a star that's twinkling down at us.

'Thank me for what?'

'For the website idea,' I tell him. 'But this morning, I thought of something else.'

'What?'

'What if we make an app instead of a website?' I wonder if he will laugh at me.

'An app?'

'Yeah. An app would be more accessible, right? We could model it after the various home service apps that are out there, but keep it simple. Simpler.'

There's silence for a few seconds. 'An app will cost a lot to make, Abir,' he says.

'I know. I know that.' I quickly tell him about the campus incubation programme and that we could work on a mock-up of sorts using free resources. We would also need to define what we want the app to look like so we can pitch it.

'That's a good idea, but . . .'

'But?' My heart sinks. I won't be able to do this without his help. In college, they're teaching us html, SQL and C++, and even so, they're just skimming the surface. There's no way I can design or figure out how to make an app. Sahil is studying software engineering, and I'm sure he knows much more than I do.

'How will we work on it? Where? And we would need to spend a bit of time together and . . .' he trails off, sounding a little embarrassed.

Arsalan would have barrelled his way through.

My spine stiffens. I don't need reminders of him.

'That's okay,' I assure him. 'You can come over at home, and we can work on it here. Ammi won't mind.'

'And she's okay?' he asks, surprised.

'Yes, she's fine,' I tell him. 'I've already cleared it with her.'

'Okay then. I'll come over tomorrow, and we can start working on it?'

'Yes, sure,' I tell him, and we end the call.

I would have liked to begin today, but I don't think Ammi would have spoken to Abbu yet. She better tell him about Sahil coming home till this project is done. I did her a solid today, saving her from lying more to Abbu and taking over the mantle of being a liar myself.

The sound of the Maghrib azan pierces through the fog in my mind. I listen to it, letting the verses soak into me. The clarity of the voice of the azan caller makes my skin erupt in goose pimples.

This has been a surreal day. But it's over now. Almost. And I'm ready for whatever tomorrow will bring me.

Bring it on.

21

Ammi is getting ready to go out when I go downstairs. She never goes out this late. Usually, her henna appointments are done well before Abbu returns home. But Abbu also isn't around.

'Where are you going? Where's Abbu?' I ask her.

Amal is at the famed dining table, doing her homework.

'He went out to meet some friends. And I have to go to apply mehendi for a bride. It was a last-minute request. It's an engagement and the mehendiwali cancelled. So they reached out to me,' Ammi says. Her bag with all her mehendi cones and patterns is slung over her shoulder.

'And Abbu? Is he going to be okay?'

Ammi looks unsure. 'I asked him about it,' she says and something inside me clenches. She could have just *told* him about it. That's what he does, doesn't he?

'And?'

'He wanted to know where and how long it would take. But I'm not sure actually,' she says, looking a little defeated.

'What? Why?'

'It's far, Abir. Nida and Samreen can't come with me. I don't feel comfortable travelling back alone,' she says.

'I'll come with you.'

Both of us are shocked. I have never accompanied Ammi. Amal had gone with her a few times in the early days when she was nine or ten, but I always preferred to stay at home with Nani, watching TV or listening to music. Also, once at a wedding, someone had referred to my mother as a mehendiwali and it had stung. In my adolescence, I had been ashamed of it—ashamed that my mother did this for money.

I was so over being that girl now. If I could go back in time, I'd probably slap myself. It had taken me a few years to look at what Ammi did in a different light. She herself considered it something she did to pass the time, when the truth was that she didn't have any time at all. And she used the money to supplement her monthly budget, buy something for us without having to worry Abbu. I don't think I've ever seen her use the money to buy anything for herself.

God, I hated that mothers were so selfless. If she was selfish, it would have sucked too, but I wanted her to strike a balance. To feel free to use the money she earned from her hard work. And today was indeed a milestone because she'd got the table repaired with her own money.

'Really?' she asks.

I nod. Seeing Ammi's henna paraphernalia has reminded me of something else. We need to revive the Instagram account and rack up some followers.

'I need to take some photos for the Instagram account,' I tell her.

'But who even sees it?' she asks. 'I think there are only four followers.'

I know. I had set up the Instagram account a couple of years ago, but I hadn't been too active on it. I never accompanied Ammi. And Ammi, Nida Phuppu and Samreen Khala never remembered to take photos of the designs once they had finished. So I didn't have enough material to post on the page, and I'd let it die away slowly.

But that's going to change. I'm going to turn things around a bit. Having a decent social media following should be good leverage for us in the pitch.

'Chalo, let's go then,' she says. 'I'm getting late.'

I grab my abaya and don it, tie a scarf around my head, and we leave. It feels odd to be travelling with Ammi. I can't plug in my earphones and listen to music as I always do because it would be rude.

'How are we going there?' I ask her.

'We'll take an auto. I'll add it to the charges,' she says.

Finally. 'Yes, please do that,' I tell her fervently.

'I also know these things, Abir,' Ammi says quietly as we get into an auto. The house is in Jayanagar, and that's very far from our home. The auto fare itself would be at least ₹200.

'Then why don't you use them?' I ask her.

'I don't want anyone to think I consider myself very important or that I take this very seriously.'

I let out a breath. I know why. Because she believes it would undermine what Abbu does for us. I'm surprised when she reaches out and squeezes my hand. Ammi is not a hugger or given to casual affectionate touches. None of us are in my family.

'You are so much like me,' she says.

I am?

She nods when she sees the confused look in my eyes, but she doesn't explain further.

'You're not the only one in this world to have rebelled, Abir,' she says mysteriously. *What?* Nani has told me so many things about Ammi, so how come I've never heard about my mother, the rebel? 'Maybe I'll tell you some day.'

Half an hour later, we are led inside the bride's room in a large, opulent house. The house has been decorated with twinkling, gaudy lights, but there's no chaos. Maybe because this is just an engagement and not a wedding.

The bride is dressed in a simple shalwar kurta, but she's fidgety and impatient. Her face breaks out into a smile when she sees us.

'Oh, thank god, there are two of you. We can be done soon,' she says.

I shoot an alarmed look at my mother, who just smiles. 'I'll be applying the mehendi,' she says in a calm voice to the bride, who looks at both of us again, as if wondering why I'm here.

'Would you be okay if I took a few photos of your henna design once it's done?' I ask her.

She frowns. 'Why?'

'I need it for our Instagram page,' I explain.

She shrugs. 'As long as you don't show my face.'

I nod, curbing the urge to tell her what I think of her face. I know why I don't go with Ammi for these things now.

Ammi settles on the bed, tucking the edges of her abaya underneath her feet as she readies herself for what promises to be an excruciating hour ahead.

I send a DM to Keerthi, linking the Instagram page. I tell her that this is my mother's business, and it would be great if she could like it. She responds immediately with a flurry of emojis and hearts. Soon she, along with a few other people she's rustled up, are following the page.

I start putting up stories along with poll stickers to get some sense of interaction from the audience. But there's no audience yet. Still, I persist.

Ammi gets distracted whenever I move the camera close to take a photo of the design and makes a 'pch' sound each time. So, I step back and sourcing photos from free photo sites, I fill up the page with a few posts. But then I look at the design that's emerging on the bride's palm, and I suppress a gasp.

I knew Ammi was talented. But this is simply magnificent.

One of the things I feel I should learn from Ammi is that she gives every job her best. She never holds back, thinking that, oh, this is just an engagement; a simpler design will be enough. Honestly, if it were me, I would do just that. I'd assess the event and maybe pull down the design by a few notches if the bride was rude or annoying. Maybe just a little more than the bare minimum.

But Ammi never would. For her, customer satisfaction and pride in her work are one and the same.

'Ammi, one photo,' I tell her. She nods, but I'm transfixed by the way the line of henna moves from the cone, almost as if it has a life of its own and she's directing it.

'*You* don't know how to apply?' the bride asks me.

Ammi shakes her head. 'No, she's still studying. Anyway, she's not meant for all this.'

The words strike something in my heart. I'm proud that Ammi thinks I'm meant for more, but I'm also sad that she thinks it's okay for her to be meant for this. Ammi could have been meant for so much more too. It just adds to my determination to give that to her, however, and whenever I can.

'You should have also learnt,' the bride says again. 'You could have helped your mother.'

'I *am* helping her,' I tell her flatly.

The bride rolls her eyes. I am very tempted to take her palms and rub them together to ruin her design, but of course that would be childish and very stupid.

To my surprise, Ammi glances up at her and shakes her head. 'Don't move, please,' she issues the directive in a curt voice.

Surprised, the bride wiggles her back. 'But my back is hurting.'

Her *back is hurting,* I think indignantly.

Ammi catches my eye over her head, and a look passes between us. Ammi knows too. That she's better than this. That the art she is creating deserves more respect.

I will make sure of that.

22

If I keep myself distracted long enough, I won't think too much about what will happen once I go inside the classroom. This is what I've been telling myself all morning after waking up from yet another weird dream.

No, I am not going to relive it or even think about it. There were no dining tables in it. Nor any Sahils.

Anyway.

I check my phone to see if there's been any magical growth on the Instagram page since last night, but of course there hasn't. This is real life, after all. Not a movie where things just work out perfectly for the protagonists. Keerthi has managed to drum up around twelve followers, but that's it.

I will need to make the account more visible somehow before it's time for the pitch.

I hitch my backpack higher and walk into the classroom. My stomach lurches in anticipation. It's not like it's my brain that I can tell it to shut up. It's biological.

I don't glance left or right as I make my way straight up the steps to where Keerthi . . . she's not there. I look around cautiously and breathe out a relieved sigh when I see that no one has noticed me come inside. *Thank god.*

Where's Keerthi? I sit down at our usual place, and my eyes scan the rows because I'm looking for Keerthi. But if she'd been sitting here, she would have called out to me already.

I check my phone to see if she's sent me any messages, and then I blink when I see a couple from Nina, the class rep. She's sent the messages early today before coming to college, and I'd somehow missed seeing them.

PCMC 22 23
Friday

Nina 5:10

Ms Kannan has banned the use of mobile phones in classrooms. Specially after photos and videos of students are being made illegally.

No. No way.

I should be glad that no one else has responded to her text, and more so that she hasn't named me, but my face heats with embarrassment anyway. I put away my phone.

Keerthi comes inside the classroom and waves at me as if she hasn't seen me in years. I wave back at her reluctantly. She comes up the steps, out of breath and she pushes me inside to sit at the very edge of the bench.

Before I can ask her anything, Arsalan walks in and strides up the steps purposefully.

I don't look at him. He doesn't look at me.

Good. We can pretend that we don't exist to each other. I can't handle the embarrassment otherwise. I mean, I can, but I'd rather not. I'd rather focus my energies on other important things.

'. . . and there's so much to tell you,' Keerthi says in a quiet voice. I haven't heard a word of what she's been telling me because I'd been so intent on ignoring Arsalan.

Ms Vishwanathan enters. The buzz in the class dies down to the usual uncomfortable silence.

I'm feeling uneasy today.

I am used to Arsalan sitting at the back, but today it feels different. My neck feels warm. I find myself sitting up straighter. I feel his eyes are on me, though I know that's not true.

My mind spins a little out of control. What happened yesterday was no big deal to him. And he got the videos deleted. I only have Keerthi's word that he deleted the videos that everyone took. Although, if he were the sort of terrible person that I think he is, he would have held on to one as some leverage against me. But then, what would that gain him? I am a nobody, and any leverage is of no value. But he could use them to make me do his assignments or he could even insist I let him copy from my . . .

I remember something else. I look around the class, taking in the people sitting, clueless about the worry that has just erupted in my head. None of them are aware of what it means to be me. It probably would not be a big deal to any of them, even if they were. Archana, the girl with whom I am usually paired in practical classes, is not here. That means that I will have to spend an hour with Arsalan again.

Last week had been bad enough. I had to control my urge to slap him when he was playing around with the acids. I should have stayed home. But that would have given the message that I was afraid to be around him. And I am fearless.

Right?

Right.

I haven't concentrated on a word of whatever is being taught today by Ms Vishwanathan.

Keerthi glances at my empty notebook and her eyes widen. 'Abir!' she whispers frantically.

'What?'

'Notes!'

'I know.'

'What will I do?' she whispers again. 'I was counting on you.'

I am not the repository of class notes. I really want to tell her that but I'm wary of putting this out in the open. Our friendship is firm and strong, but the past few days have put a different spin on many things. And I wonder if she's pissed at me for being in the video instead of her. If she's irritated that *I* fell into Arsalan's arms instead of her, well, she's more than welcome to him and his arms. But nothing can be done right now.

'I'll get the notes from someone else. Don't worry,' I tell her softly.

'Abir and Keerthi! You can share your findings with us too,' Ms Vishwanathan calls out.

'Noooooo,' Keerthi whispers, her eyes widening in shock as Ms Vishwanathan makes her way up the steps.

I'm screwed too. If she sees my empty notebook, she'll want to know what I was doing all through class. But just as she's nearing us, there's a commotion behind us. Someone falls on the steps with a thump.

Everyone turns to see what's going on. Luke is sprawled on the step near the bench where he'd been sitting with Arsalan. He looks flummoxed as he tries to stand up, but he falls again. He looks down at his shoelaces, as do we all. They've been tied together.

'Luke D'Costa! What are you doing?' Ms Vishwanathan booms, forgetting the two of us as she makes her way back. Normally, teachers are very chilled out or don't care enough to see what we're doing but not Ms Vishwanathan. She's strict, and she likes to show it.

Luke scratches his head in confusion. 'I think I tied my shoelaces by mistake.'

Everyone laughs.

'Of course you're supposed to tie your shoelaces, silly boy,' Ms Vishwanathan says.

'I mean, I've tied them together?' he says.

Again, people laugh.

Ms Vishwanathan shakes her head and walks up to him. She inspects his shoes. 'I'm going to kick you out of class for disrupting, but . . .'

The hour bell rings loudly. Students push the benches they're sitting on and stand up. The commotion is loud. Ms Vishwanathan makes a face as she walks back to the lectern and collects her things.

'That was a lucky escape!' Keerthi says, clutching my hands.

Lucky? I don't think so. I'd glanced at Arsalan a few seconds ago when everyone had been looking at Luke, and he'd lifted an eyebrow.

He'd even mouthed, 'You're welcome.'

23

I don't see why we need to work in pairs in the chemistry laboratory or any lab for that matter. I think we're perfectly capable of doing the experiments on our own. In fact, having someone else hover nearby is more likely to cause accidents in the lab.

My entire body feels like a chemistry experiment. Some parts of it are hot, and some parts are cold—which makes no sense whatsoever. And I'm entirely too aware of my cellular structure.

Arsalan is next to me, all tall and lithe. I feel like a mushroom in comparison. I am going to strangle Archana the next time she decides to bunk college on a day we have practicals.

Keerthi looks at me across the lab and waves. Then she makes eyes in Arsalan's direction and grins at me. Like I'm supposed to enjoy his company.

'Students, titration carries ten marks in the practical exam,' Ms Ahuja intones. Someone giggles because she pronounces it as 'tit-ration', and of course, our class has a bunch of idiot boys who will find it funny.

She sniffles, ignoring them, and goes on to explain how we are supposed to conduct the experiment. I try my best to focus on her instructions and manage perfectly well until I hear some humming behind us. My face flames when I realize that they're humming 'Suraj Hua Maddham'.

'Ignore them,' Arsalan says quietly.

'Easy for you to say!' I lash out with gritted teeth. I glance up in his direction and then look away quickly because he's looking at me, and I can't seem to level my gaze with his. I want to be anywhere but here. I need to be somewhere stable because right now, it feels like the ground is tilting.

'I wanted to apologize to you the other day, but you'd already left,' he says.

I look down at the burette and pick it up, inspecting it this way and that in unnecessary detail, trying not to let his words affect me.

'If you don't follow my instructions, the tit-ration will not work,' Ms Ahuja calls out. 'You have to weigh the oxalic acid at exactly 3.15 grams.'

'Why are you apologizing?' I ask with a frown.

He shrugs. 'I don't know. I just felt like I should.'

'Unless you got some of your minions to make it in the first place?' *Of course. That makes more sense.*

'Wow. Your opinion of me is unbelievably low,' he mutters.

113

'Well, you haven't given me any reason to think otherwise,' I retort.

'Exactly what have I done to get this reaction from you?' he asks.

This time, when I look at him, I don't look away. My stomach flips.

'You make fun of everyone,' I point out. 'And you make beer jokes with my name.'

'You have to heat the mixture to 60 degrees before the tit-ration,' Ms Ahuja says. 'I will be coming around to check.'

The two of us work in silence for a little while. I know I've missed a step or two because I've been so distracted.

'Why do we add sulphuric acid and not any other acids like nitric acid or hydrochloric acid?' Ms Ahuja asks.

One of the front benchers, who is somewhere at the back of the lab because seats are assigned in alphabetical order, raises her hand in the air, like Hermione from the Harry Potter movies. She even waves her hand to try to get Ms Ahuja's attention.

Ms Ahuja looks everywhere but at her. Her gaze falls on us.

'You, Ass-alan. Tell me,' she says.

'Shit,' he mutters under his breath. 'I've no idea.'

Ms Ahuja is a no-nonsense teacher, and his charms don't work on her. It's one of the reasons I enjoy her class because she seems to enjoy taking him down a peg or two.

'I suppose I should thank you for getting rid of the video,' I tell him grudgingly.

'Huh?' he asks, confused.

This is my chance to clear my dues. 'Nitric acid is an oxidizing agent,' I whisper. Clearing his throat, he repeats that out loud.

Ms Ahuja looks pissed that he knows the answer. She narrows her eyes. 'And hydrochloric acid?' she asks.

'It reacts with potassium permanganate to give chlorine, which is an oxidizing agent,' I whisper, and he moves closer to catch it. His arm brushes mine, and it makes me feel lightheaded. The smell of his cologne adds to the strange chemical reactions bubbling inside me, drying my mouth.

He looks at me for a brief second, almost apologetically, and then turns to Ms Ahuja. 'I'm sorry. I don't know, ma'am.' He probably didn't hear my whisper.

This pleases her for some reason. 'You. Abeer. Do you know?'

God only knows why I've taken leave of my senses. Because I say the same thing. 'I don't know.'

She looks surprised at this and then stares at the two of us standing together. Arsalan has moved away, but my heart is still thudding so loudly.

Fool. Idiot. What's wrong with you?

'Who can tell me?' she asks, looking around. She finally spots the front bencher waving frantically. 'Yes, Neeraja. You. Tell me now.'

While Neeraja rattles off the answer, Arsalan looks at me, surprised. 'You knew the answer,' he whispers, almost accusingly.

'Yeah, I don't know what happened,' I mutter.

I *know* what happened. I've temporarily taken leave of my senses. Anyway, it's okay. These are just routine questions, and it's not like she'll deduct our marks or anything.

'Good,' Ms Ahuja says, and then turns to us. 'Assalan and Abeer will stay back and clean the equipment after the practical is over.'

What? No. Noooooooo.

24

There must be some truth to what people say about associating with the wrong kind of people. Just being in Arsalan's orbit has resulted in a video of me being made into an Instagram reel, a teacher thinking that I'm no good at studies and landing me a punishment.

It's no good that Arsalan is also included in the punishment. I'd thought he would leave all the cleaning up to me while he lounged around lazily. When I glance at him, he's going about wiping the beakers diligently with a rag.

He looks at me. The test tube in my hand nearly slips and falls. I grab it quickly. He smirks. I glare.

'To continue our conversation,' he says.

'What conversation?' I mumble as I place the test tubes in their holders and wipe the counter clean. My nose feels twitchy because of all the sharp smells. And do chemistry teachers make hydrogen sulphide every day? Because that rotten egg smell is certainly coming from somewhere here.

'About why you dislike me so much,' he says, wiping down a Bunsen burner and turning to me. He flips the rag over one shoulder, and it is annoyingly, disarmingly charming. This is the sort of move I would never have expected from someone like him. He's always so suave and put-together. An unbidden image of how he'd looked in the black pathani blazes through my mind.

'I don't dislike you,' I reply, looking away.

'Oh, so you like me then,' comes the reply almost immediately in a teasing tone.

'I never said that,' I tell him hotly. 'I'm indifferent to you.'

'That's why you make arse jokes with my name then?' he prods.

I look back at him, irritated. I try not to notice how good looking he is. 'I only do that because you make jokes with my name.'

He shrugs. 'It's too tempting.'

'Same with your name.'

At that, he grins. I find yet another wall crumbling somewhere. 'I really wish parents didn't do this.'

'What? Name us?' I ask. I find myself enjoying the banter, and I have to remind myself of who he is.

'Give us names that can be twisted and made fun of,' he says. 'I wish my father hadn't been so preoccupied with C.S. Lewis.'

My confusion is apparent, so he elaborates—'Aslan, Arsalan, both variations of the same name, right?'

Since I have no clue what he's talking about, I go back to drying the beakers and arranging them on the table.

'You don't know what I'm talking about?' he asks, almost disbelievingly.

'What's the big deal?'

'You haven't watched the Narnia movies then?' he asks.

I shrug. 'I don't remember. I'm not into movies.'

'Books?' he persists.

I turn to him, annoyed. 'What's it to you? What's with the inquisition?'

'Nothing, nothing,' he mutters as he tugs off the rag from his shoulder. He has a half-smile on his face, which is annoying because it's like he's secretly laughing at me. Maybe he is.

'I'm done here. Lock up once you're done and hand over the keys to Ms Ahuja in the staffroom,' I tell him, glad to be getting away.

'Hey, wait up for a bit,' he says, looking back at me. 'I need to talk to you.'

Something coils in my belly. 'What?'

'It's about the pitch from yesterday,' he says.

Relieved and also oddly disappointed, I nod. 'Yeah, what about it?'

He drops the rag in the dustbin and then turns around to look at the lab. We've definitely left it cleaner than it had been when we came. I hope Ms Ahuja doesn't think of making us clean again.

'What did you think about it?' he asks, looking at me intently.

My blood hums at being the focus of his attention. I can't even make my mind scoff at myself. 'Do you want my candid opinion or my candied opinion?'

He looks at me, puzzled, and then a look of delight crosses his face as he puts his head back and laughs. 'That's too good!'

'I know,' I tell him loftily, stupidly pleased at making him laugh.

'Well? I don't want the *candied* opinion,' he says as he walks towards the door.

I walk faster, so I'm outside before him. 'Okay, so your pitch sucks. There's no clear outline of the science behind it or of how you plan to achieve it. You need to be able to show them it has a sound basis and is doable. Not something that's fantastical. I thought I made it clear yesterday itself.'

His face falls, and he nods gravely. 'I knew it. I shouldn't have gone ahead with Luke's idiotic plan.'

'So? Come up with something else,' I tell him as he fits the padlock over the latch and turns the key.

'Ha. As if it's that easy. Today is the last day to register,' he adds.

'What? Today?' I nearly yell. Why hadn't I bothered to check all these details? What would have been the point of working with Sahil if I had been unable to enter the competition?

'Yeah, why?' he asks, cocking his head a little.

My face flushes. I debate telling him my plan. I shouldn't tell him about it.

Right? Right.

'Nothing. Just like that,' I tell him, although I'm bursting with the need to tell him my idea. It's not like he'd steal it. Imagine Arsalan pitching for a henna app. The thought makes me grin involuntarily, but he doesn't notice. I sober up immediately.

He nods. A different look comes into his eyes, one that I can't decipher. 'It's just that I'd hoped to do something big. To achieve something with our idea.'

He looks a little lost.

I ask him. 'Why?'

What does it even matter to him? He's rich as Midas, I'm sure.

'What do you mean, why?'

'I mean, what does it matter to you?'

We're walking towards the staff room. I'm grateful no one stood outside the lab to hum some idiotic song or the other.

'Why *wouldn't* it matter to me?' he asks, baffled.

I can't explain it to him. It makes me wonder if Keerthi is right. That I am a reverse snob. Just because he's rich doesn't mean that he doesn't want to do something on his own.

But then, what's to stop him from doing that anyway? I'm sure his father will bankroll him. Once he finishes college, he'll make millions with whatever start-up he decides to set up. That's the sort of privilege I'm up against. And it doesn't make me feel any better that I'll always be on the outside of such opportunities, against people like him who have generational wealth.

I just need to think about all these things, and whatever strange attraction I feel for Arsalan will vanish. I feel better already.

'You didn't answer, Abir,' he says in a low voice.

Of course, the strange attraction hasn't gone anywhere. I'm deluding myself if I think that whatever this is I'm feeling has dissipated. My body reacts as if his words were an actual caress.

I'm disgusted with myself. I stop and turn around.

'You're super rich. Everyone knows that. So whatever you're doing, it's because you *want* to do it, not because you *have* to do it, like some of us.' My face flushes as I speak, but I need to get the words out. 'And in the same way, if you don't succeed in this, what does it even matter? I'm sure your father will help you with whatever you need to, once you finish college. How does a little piddly competition matter to you? Unless you're competitive for the sake of being competitive?'

He stares at me in silence, his tight jaw the only indication that my words are affecting him. He reaches out and picks up my hand.

What's he doing? What's he doing?

He puts the keys in my upturned palm and walks away.

25

I'm going to blame my temporary insanity on the fumes I inhaled in the chemistry lab. Because there's no other explanation.

I run after Arsalan. I am aware that the lunch break is about to end and the next class will begin. But I need to talk to him.

'Arsalan! Wait up,' I call out.

He doesn't pause, but his stride has slowed.

I hurry up towards him. 'Hey,' I tell him when I'm standing in front of him, panting a little.

What am I doing? This is totally a mistake. Abort! Abort!

I don't know who has taken up residence in my head (the same entity who has been supplying me with those strange dreams, I guess). I look up at his blank face.

'What is it?' he asks. 'You made it clear what you think about me. So why are you here?'

'I . . .'

This is a dumb idea. Why on *earth* would he want to join my team? I don't even have a team as such, although I know I can count on Keerthi to join.

He'll laugh at my idea like I laughed at his.

'I'm sorry,' I tell him.

He shrugs. 'Okay.'

He moves as if to leave, and I step out of his way, feeling even more foolish. I straighten my spine at the errant thought. I, Abir Maqsood, am not foolish. Ever. And that's why I don't invite Arsalan to join my team. He'd never fit in. He'd think it silly.

'Where do we have to register for the incubation programme?' I ask. I don't need to ask him. I can find out myself. But my mouth apparently has a mind of its own.

'Do I look like an information desk to you?' he asks, folding his arms.

I exhale softly. 'Wow, back to being an arse. Thanks for reminding me.' I back away, feeling slightly better. The world was off kilter when I thought I liked him.

I walk away. Nothing good could have come of this irritable obsession that seems to be growing in my mind.

'Registration is in the admin building,' he calls out.

I give him a middle-finger salute without turning around.

After handing over the keys, I head to the admin building, where an irate receptionist asks me where

I want to go. She has no clue about the incubation programme, but she calls someone to find out. When she hangs up, she nods her head in the direction where I'm supposed to go.

I finally find myself at a desk, where I have to pay, fill out a form and enter details about my class and admission number. The man glances at my form without even a flicker of interest.

'Is today the last day for registration?'

He nods.

'And when will we know? When will we have to pitch?'

'Sometime next month. That will be the college round. Ten days after that, if your pitch is selected, then you have to present before the jury.'

Feeling a jolt of excitement, I nod. He sees my expression and rolls his eyes. 'We should rename our city from Garden City to Start-up City, no?'

I don't want to offend him, but I can't help myself. 'Bangalore is already the start-up capital of India.'

His expression turns blank, and he nods at me as if to say, go along, go along. 'Aal the best,' he says.

I feel a burst of energy inside me. I have a good feeling about this.

I hurry to look for Keerthi as the bell rings. Lunch is over. Keerthi won't answer if I call her because, like everyone else, her phone will be silent in college.

Our next class is maths. I make my way to the classroom where a good number of people are converging. I spot Keerthi from behind and call out to her.

She turns around, smiles and hangs back until I can join her.

'Well?' she asks, her eyes alight.

'I just signed us up for the campus incubation programme!'

Her eyes dim. 'What?'

'Yeah. What were you so excited about? You'll join my team, right? I need help with the pitch and everything.'

'Yeah, that's okay, but I meant what happened with Arsalan?' she asks in a hushed whisper.

Blotches of colour appear on my cheeks.

Her eyes widen. 'Ooh! Look at your face!'

'Shut up. Nothing happened. Why would it?' I ask her.

'I mean, come on!' she says, grinning.

'We cleaned the lab, and I handed over the keys to Ms Ahuja. That's it.'

'That's it, she says,' Keerthi repeats in a stage whisper.

'Arrey. What can happen in a chemistry lab? We're surrounded by chemicals and acids.'

'What did you sign us up for?' she asks, thankfully dropping the topic.

'The henna app I was telling you about earlier,' I tell her, as we enter the classroom. 'Today was the last day to register.'

The moment we step inside, a bunch of boys stand up, put their hands on their hearts, and start singing: *'Hum tum ek kamre mein band ho, aur chaabi kho jaaye.'*

Arsalan is sitting in his usual spot, a smirk on his face, and this time, he gives me a middle-finger salute.

26

I am cold and poised through the rest of the college day. My focus is sharp and unwavering in class. Inside, I feel anger, fury and everything in between.

I shouldn't have let my guard down. Thank god I didn't ask him to join my team. Or he might have got the boys to sing 'Mehendi Laga ke Rakhna' when I entered the classroom.

When it's time to go home, I tell Keerthi that I'll call her and update her about the henna app. She nods unhappily. I finally get out of my own shell and ask her what's wrong.

'You'll miss your bus,' she says as we stand near the gates.

I know Arsalan will be driving past soon enough, and I want to leave before I do something unforgivable like throw a rock at his car.

'It's okay,' I tell Keerthi, steering her away from the gate.

I realize that I am often a selfish friend, hardly ever bothering to listen to anyone else's problems because mine seem so huge and insurmountable. I wonder if she sees me as someone so occupied with her own issues that she can't see what others are going through at all.

Keerthi says. 'It's silly.'

'So? Tell me about it. Friends are for sharing all these silly things.'

In the distance, I can see Arsalan getting into his car. He and Luke are backslapping each other. He must be laughing at how he got the last word. Forget a rock. I wish there were a pat of cow dung somewhere. I'd have flung it at his windshield.

'I just realized that Arsalan is such a douchebag,' she says.

I burst out laughing involuntarily. 'What?'

She nods. 'All these days I thought that he just behaves this way, and he's probably a sweet guy, but what he did to you today . . .'

I feel a surge of affection for her. I thought she'd never take off her rose-tinted glasses where he was concerned.

'It's okay. I'll live,' I tell her wryly.

'You really are something else, you know,' Keerthi says, squeezing my hand. 'I would have run away from there crying.'

'I thought about it. But what would that achieve? And I can't miss classes, man. I have to ace my exams. Everything in my future hinges on it.'

She sighs. 'Give me half of your drive, no?'

'Give me half of your wealth, no?'

We both burst out laughing.

'It's true. You have to struggle in life to have this sort of relentless drive to succeed,' I tell her gently. 'I'm not saying that people who have it easy don't struggle. But it's a different ball game for us.'

She looks at me thoughtfully. And then her attention is drawn to the car that's driving out. 'We should do something,' she mutters.

'What?'

'Maybe puncture his tyres or something.'

'Eh, please. I don't have the time for all that. Honestly. The best revenge is to succeed and get ahead in life. And I have plans. A five-year, ten-year and fifteen-year plan for my life.'

Keerthi looks at me, eyes wide. 'What? Who *are* you? Who even does that?'

I shrug. 'My mother disregards all my plans because all she can see is getting me married after I finish college.'

Keerthi claps her hand over her mouth. 'Married?' she asks in horror.

'Oh, that's common. So many girls finish college just as a rite of passage and not for anything else. But not me,' I tell her softly.

'What will you do? You'll go against your family?' she asks curiously.

The car is drawing nearer. I can see Arsalan behind the wheel. There's no smirk on his face, not that I'm looking that carefully or anything.

'No, I'll convince them of what's right for me.'

'And what if they don't agree?'

'They will.'

The car is nearer. Both of us look up as he passes.

Keerthi surprises me by lifting both her hands and flashing her middle fingers up prominently. 'Fool!' she shouts.

Arsalan is momentarily startled, but I look away. The car exits the gates, and I giggle.

'That felt good,' Keerthi mutters.

'I almost told him about the henna app,' I tell her.

'What? Why? Thank god, you didn't!' she says, clutching my hand.

'We got talking in the chem lab and he seemed nice. Fun, even. And he was a bit sad about not pitching for that dumb idea with Luke.' I glance at my watch.

'I'll walk you to the bus stop, and you can tell me all about it,' she says.

We leave college. I've always felt a sense of exhilaration while walking in through these gates every morning. This is my gateway to better things in life. All the cribbing and moaning about exams, classes and practicals aside, college is the way my life is going to change for the better. And when I leave the gates in the evening, I can't wait to come back the next day.

No guy is going to change that for me. Arsalan can come up with a thousand different ways to humiliate me, but I don't care. If I repeat that often enough, I'll maybe believe it eventually.

'So? What happened? You guys were going to become friends, and then he pulled that stunt?' Keerthi asks.

I give her a brief summary of what I told him and that he'd looked hurt. So I'd chased after him to ask him to join my team, but I stopped myself at the last moment.

She nods thoughtfully. 'So he was retaliating then,' she says as if it makes sense.

'Whatever. I don't care. I don't have time for these childish games,' I tell her.

Keerthi looks at me in wonder. 'You guys,' she whispers.

'What?'

'You know, I had a small crush on him that he wiped out today after what he did to you. But you two . . . It's the perfect enemies-to-lovers story!'

My heart jumps at the word 'lovers' but I keep my face straight. 'A what?'

'You know, enemies-to-lovers is a thing. A proper thing in books and movies.' She rattles off a number of titles, none of which I've heard. When she sees the blank look on my face, she clutches my wrist in irritation. 'Have you been living under a rock?'

I nod. 'Yeah, I have. And I'm staying right inside.'

27

The next morning in college, Keerthi hands me her Kindle with all the books she had downloaded. When I tell her I don't have time to read them, she insists I take it home with me.

'Return my Kindle once you finish reading *all* these books,' she tells me. 'First, read *Pride and Prejudice*.'

I have no intention of reading even one. *How will she even know?*

The following day, when I hand it back to her, she rolls her eyes.

'No. Do yourself and myself and everyone else a favour and read these,' she says, giving it right back.

'Why would I be doing everyone and myself a favour?' I ask her, frowning.

'You might learn to be a little less crabby once you lose yourself in the world of romance,' she says loftily. 'This is my spare Kindle. You can keep it for as long as you want.'

I don't light into her for that. Because, despite myself, last night I'd started reading *The Hating Game,* and I was hooked. I'd stayed up till 1 a.m. reading.

Amal had been shocked to see me read fiction, especially on a Kindle. When I told her it belonged to my friend who loaned it for me to read some books, she turned green with envy.

'You can read on it when the lights are off, and it won't ruin your eyes,' she mumbled. 'And you can read on the bus. Doesn't hurt your eyes as much as reading printed paper.'

I immediately decide to save up to buy one for her for her birthday.

I find myself picking up the Kindle whenever I have some spare time. And before I know it, I'd read three romances. Some of the stories seem predictable, but I enjoy how the resolution comes about. I have my own inner monologue with the heroines at times, and sometimes I want to yell at them for being foolish.

Keerthi and I discuss some of these books. Sometimes, she looks at me almost expectantly.

I don't talk about Arsalan at all. Whatever tentative friendship there had been has been obliterated — by his actions and, I have to admit, by my own high-handed behaviour.

I'm a little confused because Keerthi never brings him up in conversation directly. But he's there nevertheless, like some sort of cloud hanging over us. He's there in person too, but I've done by my best to ignore him. And he's ignored me too.

That's a relief. Yes, it is absolutely a relief. I mean it.

'So, what's happening with the henna app?' Keerthi asks me, a week later.

'Don't ask,' I groan, covering my face with my hands.

All my big ideas had been hinged on getting Sahil's help. But when Ammi finally and hesitantly brought it up with Abbu, he didn't understand.

'Why does he need to come here?' he glowered.

'I need his help in working on the prototype of an app I'm making,' I told him.

But the words made no sense to Abbu. 'Why do you need his help? Why can't you find it on the internet?' Abbu's temper could be volcanic, and I didn't want to be at the receiving end.

Ammi finally managed to convince Abbu that only Sahil could help me out. He came home last evening. Abbu sat at the dining table, scowling at both of us, as if he was waiting for Sahil to make one wrong move and he would have him by the throat.

I could hardly talk or explain to him what needed to be done because I was so aware of Abbu's gaze on us. Sahil left half an uncomfortable hour later, and I felt despair loom over me. This was never going to work out. My app would never get made, and I would not be able to pitch it.

Keerthi looks disappointed. 'No! The app is such a good idea. We need to make this happen!'

'But how,' I tell her, clutching my head. 'We need to make the framework for the app. I need someone with some coding expertise at least. I can't do it on my own.'

135

She looks thoughtful.

We are waiting for the next teacher to show up. The class is abuzz as usual with something or the other. The back of my neck feels hot. Arsalan is sitting somewhere behind us.

'I have an idea,' she says suddenly.

'What?'

'We can work on the app at my place after college,' she says. 'And we'll call Sahil there.'

A bubble of hope grows inside. 'I might be able to pull it off once, Keerthi. Coming over to your house, I mean. But beyond that, Ammi might not like it.'

'Tell her we're studying for exams,' she says. She sees my face and exclaims. 'For the love of god, Abir. It's not like you're going off somewhere with a guy. You'll be *working* on something. What can be the problem with that?'

She's right. But I don't like the idea of lying to my mother. Still, I have to think of the larger picture, and I think it makes sense.

'Okay,' I tell her, a little excited. 'Okay.'

I have to tell Ammi that I can get the work done without Sahil's help after all. She'll be relieved about that. And without Abbu's presence, we might get something done.

'Text Sahil. I'll send you my address, and you forward it to him,' Keerthi says.

'Yes, boss!' I tell her with a big grin. *This is finally happening!*

28

'**B**ut why do you need to study at her house?' Ammi sounds baffled when I call to tell her the plan.

'She needs my help, Ammi.'

I have the insane urge to go home, as always. My feet are almost carrying me towards the gate of their own accord.

'Why does it have to be you?'

'Ammi, there's not much time left before exams. She's worried she'll fail.' I wince at the fib. Keerthi's not bad at studies.

'Hmm. Okay. Helping your friends is important too. But what about that thing with Sahil?' Ammi asks.

'I'm trying to see if I can do it myself. Keerthi says she can help.'

'What? She needs your help in studies, but this complicated computer coding thing and all, she can do?' Ammi sounds confused.

'Yeah,' I try to sound convincing. 'So we'll get both done at the same time.'

'Okay, Abir. Try not to be too late.'

I end the call as Keerthi comes running towards me.

'All set?' she asks breathlessly. 'Cool. Let's go. Our ride is ready.'

Like a fool, I thought she meant an Uber. Because she leads me to the car, where Arsalan is waiting outside the driver's door, a pair of sunglasses hanging off his fingers.

My first incoherent thought is that his face does not look as sweaty and oily as mine feels.

'Keerthi! What are you doing?' I ask her in a horrified whisper.

'Arsalan offered to drop us home,' she says as if it's perfectly normal.

I stare at her with gritted teeth. 'What did you do?'

'Look, you and I need someone like him.'

I stare at her. 'What do you mean? Why do we need him?'

'For the pitch. He'll be useful, ya,' she says in a low voice.

'You told him about the pitch?'

She shakes her head. 'No, but you will. I just asked him if he wants to join our team, and he said yes.'

I wanted to tell her that *she* was no longer part of the team. But then she's offering her house and

I need it. Why on earth did she think involving Arsalan was a good idea?

'I know you're mad,' she says as we walk closer to the car.

Arsalan is wearing the shades now. I can't discern his expression as he gets into the driver's seat. I feel mortified. What must he be thinking of all this?

She invited the enemy to join the team. She thinks that Arsalan and I are going to become an enemies-to-lovers thing.

I'm going to kill her.

She opens the front passenger seat and indicates that I should sit there. If I refuse, it will look churlish. I don't want to make a scene. I feel like I've set in motion something that's not going to be easy to get out of. But what can I do now? How do I extricate myself from this situation?

My heart is thumping as I slide into the seat. I hope that my deo is still working. I can't smell any B.O.

I sit like a statue, staring straight ahead. Keerthi gets into the back seat.

Arsalan starts the car and drives out of college. I try hard not to stare at the way his forearms flex.

'Have you sent my address to Sahil?' Keerthi pipes up.

'Who's Sahil?' Arsalan asks.

'He's helping me with the app,' I tell him without looking at him. His eyes are on the road. 'I'm sending it to him now.'

139

'He's okay with this, right?' Keerthi asks.

'I don't know. I'll have to ask him once he comes there.'

'So he's like a computer geek?' Arsalan asks.

My jaw works, but I nod. 'Yeah. He's studying software engineering, and he knows this stuff.'

'So, listen, Abir, um, thanks for taking me on the team,' Arsalan says, looking a little bashful.

'What's your angle?' I blurt out immediately.

I hear a slapping sound behind us. Keerthi must be face-palming.

'Angle?' he asks, frowning.

'Yeah. Why would you join my team?'

'Right, I forgot you have a very low opinion of me,' he mutters as he changes gears. *Why does that look so sexy? I need to get my head checked.*

'Look, I already told you that I want to pitch. I think it is a fabulous learning opportunity. When Keerthi asked if I wanted to join your team, I agreed without even hearing what the idea was. Your idea is guaranteed to be way better than Luke's. I want to help.'

I fold my arms and sit back. Maybe I'm reading more into this than there actually is. Why can't I take anything at face value? I school my features into a more pleasant expression.

'Are you in pain?' Arsalan asks, sounding concerned.

Keerthi leans forward. 'What happened, Abir? Cramps? Periods?'

I groan. 'No. I'm fine. I was just trying to think of how to explain the project to you.'

'Easy. Just tell him what you told me,' Keerthi says.

I turn my head back so fast, I'm sure I have whiplash and glare at her.

'It's an app for henna,' I say.

'What?' he barks, disbelief evident in his voice.

'See?' I tell Keerthi. 'He doesn't like it.'

'I didn't say that. Explain your plan,' he says quickly.

I shut my eyes, thinking of the way my mother massaged her fingers that night. Of how tired she looked. Of how defeated she'd seemed when Champagne Saree hadn't paid her, her dues.

'It's a home service app. But for henna.'

'Go on,' he says with an encouraging smile.

Steeling myself, I start talking.

29

When Arsalan smiles at me, it feels like something out of an alien movie—when the extraterrestrial pops out of the human's body. Then, as he keeps smiling, a jolt of warmth coasts through me, making the tips of my fingers and toes tingle and filling me with a strange sense of longing.

When we reach Keerthi's house, she directs him to the visitor parking. I look around, stunned. This is a gated villa property. We have to walk a small distance to her villa from the parking lot. We pass by a sparkling blue swimming pool. Keerthi waves at someone who is walking in the other direction, and he waves back at her.

'There's a park through there,' Keerthi says, pointing to a trellised archway wrapped with green vines. The air feels different—less dusty, more green.

'Nice place,' Arsalan says.

He probably lives somewhere like this too.

'Thanks,' Keerthi says. 'Oops!'

'What?' I ask.

'I have to tell the security uncle to let Sahil through,' she says. 'Why don't the two of you wait by that bench over there? I'll quickly go tell him.'

I start saying that I also want to come with her, but she's gone. What does she think will happen in the five minutes she's gone?

'Shall we?' Arsalan asks, indicating the bench.

'No thanks. I'm good,' I tell him.

He walks ahead. It feels odd to be just standing around. So I follow him. He slows his stride to match mine.

'I've been meaning to apologize to you about that day,' he says.

I shrug. We walk to the bench, and he sits down with a thump.

'Come on. Just for a bit,' he says.

I sit down too, keeping my distance from him. It feels strange — good strange, I guess?

'It feels good to stretch your legs,' he says, extending his long legs.

I stare at them before looking away. When he crosses his arms across his chest, I can see his biceps pop out. Oddly, I don't feel as irritated by the sight as I used to.

'So who else is at home, Abir?' he asks. 'Asoda? Awhisky?'

'Ha ha.' I roll my eyes.

He grins, and the sight makes something catch in my chest. 'Sorry. Sorry. I promised I wouldn't make fun of your name again,' he says.

'I don't know if you're any good at keeping promises though,' I blurt out.

He pauses. 'I guess I deserved that. I was pissed that day. You were making some really terrible assumptions about me. Then you gave that speech about how I didn't *need* to do anything and that got me mad.'

'Isn't it true, though?' I ask after a moment or two. I know he's still looking at me.

'It isn't,' he says, looking at me squarely.

'What do you mean?'

'My father didn't grow up rich. He was from a middle-class family. He worked hard and made all his money. So it's not like we grew up swimming in wealth,' he says.

'Like Scrooge McDuck.'

He looks startled and then laughs. 'You've seen that show?'

I nod.

'So, yeah, Abbu wants me to work hard and make my own way into the world. It's not like he won't help me if I ask, but he'd be disappointed. He wants me to build something on my own. So, maybe some of what you said is right. Having a rich father might help me out, but I don't want it to. I want to do whatever it is on my own.'

He says this with such sincerity that I feel an answering spark inside. One that grows into a flame that I have no clue how to tamp down.

Our gazes snag and hold. And neither of us looks away. It's scary. It's exhilarating. *I want to go home. I never want to leave this bench.*

'I have a sister. Her name is Amal.' I tell him. 'You?'

'The same. One sister,' he says.

This is not the time for an epiphany.

What I have now is a full-blown crush. On Arsalan.

Kill me already.

30

Keerthi brings Sahil back with her. I walk alongside Sahil as Keerthi leads us to her villa, with Arsalan beside her.

'What's with the change of plans?' Sahil asks. He smiles at me, and there's a light in his eyes.

'You saw how it was at my home. We'd never get anything done,' I tell him. 'Is it too much of a hassle for you to come here?'

He shakes his head. 'Not really. I have my motorbike. But I might not be able to make it every day. Who's the guy?'

'He's a classmate.'

Sahil nods but looks at Arsalan speculatively.

Keerthi unlocks the door, and we step inside. 'I'm home!' she calls out.

A woman pops her head out from somewhere. She has a book in her hands and is dressed in pastel pink pants and a top in some silky material. Her reading glasses are perched on top of her head. I can see that it's Keerthi's mother.

She smiles widely. 'Keerthi! You're home? And who are your friends? Hello!'

'Friends from college, Ma. We're working on a project. Don't disturb us, okay?' Keerthi says.

I gape. She's not going to face an inquisition about who we are?

Keerthi waves her arm towards the sofas. 'Boys, just make yourself comfortable. Sahil, do you have your laptop? You can get started. Ma, give him the WiFi password.'

Sahil gives her an assessing look, which she ignores as she drags me by the elbow into her room and shuts the door.

'Well? What happened?' she whispers, her eyes as large as tennis balls. 'You two were looking quite cosy on the bench.'

'Are you insane? You have to stop doing this. Stop pushing us together like that!' A frisson of something goes up my spine when I say 'us'.

Keerthi claps her hands. 'OMG yes. There's an us!'

I take a moment to calm myself and take in her room as she twirls in the middle of it. There are hardwood floors, a full-length mirror and a full wall of wardrobes. The walls are mint green and the windows are huge. I can imagine Ammi tut-tutting about how risky they were because they were made of glass with no grilles and how any burglar can come waltzing inside.

Oddly, I don't feel any envy. Even in my dreams, I know this can't be my life.

'I got you inside to ask you what happened at the bench. You two were talking very intently.'

'We talked about our siblings,' I say.

Keerthi looks disappointed, but then cheers up. 'Let's go out and see if the boys have killed each other already.'

'You are terrible!' I tell her, feeling a jolt of affection amid the exasperation and annoyance.

'You should have seen the murderous glance Arsalan was giving Sahil,' she says gleefully. 'And you never told me Sahil was this cute.' She bumps her elbow into mine.

'I told you, but . . .'

'But now your heart beats only for Arsalan,' she says dramatically. She pauses and then says, 'Arsalan came to me the other day and told me that he wanted to apologize to you for making those boys sing the song. I told him to eat dirt.'

'What?' A laugh chokes in my throat. 'You said what?'

'I wanted to tell him to eat something a lot worse, but he already looked miserable, and I think he wanted to make amends.'

I have been through so many emotions today, and this bit of news does more strange things to my insides. I frankly don't know how to deal with all of it. 'Come, let's go out.'

We step outside to a strange tableau. Keerthi's mother is sitting on one sofa in the living room, looking in turn at the two boys, who are sitting stiffly on two facing sofas. Sahil has his laptop out and is peering at it. Arsalan looks as if he doesn't know what to do.

Keerthi finally introduces us to her mother. Despite the living room being three times the size of ours, there's a comfortable lived-in feeling. Keerthi insists all of us sit on the carpet and makes pleading faces at her mother. 'We're hungry!'

'I'm not hungry,' I tell her automatically. Years of conditioning from my parents about accepting hospitality from someone when I can't repay it come to the fore.

'That's ridiculous. You're going to shut up, and you're going to eat whatever Ma gets for us,' Keerthi says firmly.

Aunty gets up to make some sandwiches for us.

My gaze snags with Sahil's. He looks uncomfortable. At least, Arsalan and I are Keerthi's classmates.

I move closer to him. 'Do you think we can make this work? A framework, a prototype that shows how the app is meant to work?' I ask him in a low voice.

'With dummy data?'

'Yes, a dummy database. Maybe hard code it with an XML file? Then so that we can show the workings of the app—when we click on it, it populates with some sort of data,' I suggest.

I glance at Keerthi who is staring back at me as if *I* have aliens sprouting from my body now. Arsalan's face is blank. Well, this is my app, after all. I've been researching on how to create a prototype, and while we *can* create it using simple HTML, I'd rather go all out and give it our best shot.

'So we won't need to connect to a backend server during the pitch?' Sahil asks, and my attention is back on him once more.

'No, ideally, we just want to show them the workflow. So that if we open it up during the pitch, the audience can see how the user interface looks, how a user can book an appointment, and then they can pay for it using a payment gateway, and then an artist is allocated to them.'

Sahil looks mildly impressed because when he had suggested the website back in his house, it had been a less sophisticated version of this. But I've been working on what I want from the app, and I know that if I want the pitch to succeed then we have to make it look as professional as possible.

'So do you know Java or Python?' he asks.

Arsalan clears his throat. I know a little Java. Tell me what needs to be done,' he says, inching closer.

Sahil's laptop is on the coffee table, and Arsalan looks at the screen as if he can understand what's there. I tamp down the flare of resentment that he knows Java, because it's good he can help.

Keerthi nudges me. 'Pissing contest has begun,' she whispers in my ear.

31

We've all grown a little less wary of each other. The food — sandwiches and brownies — helped. Sahil and Arsalan are being extremely polite around each other, so much so that it's hilarious.

We've accomplished quite a few things.

Sahil explains that we don't need an architecture-level diagram at this step. What we need is a prototype that shows how the app will work.

'Don't we need to decide if the app is for Apple or Android or both?' Keerthi asks.

Sahil shrugs. 'All that is for later. We don't have to decide any of that yet. We just need to have a design and a framework with a user interface in place.'

They turn to me. They want to know my vision for the app and how much they can achieve while writing the code. I really wish we didn't have to take Sahil's help, and I had the means and the skills to do it on my own. But this is going to have to be a collaborative effort as much as it pains me.

Ideas and suggestions come thick and fast. I'm so engrossed that I completely forget to check my phone. When I do check, I'm shocked to see that two hours have passed.

My heart races when I see the number of missed calls blinking on my screen. I'd forgotten to unmute my phone after leaving college. Five from my mother, two from Amal, and one from Abbu.

Shit. Shit.

I jump up and begin collecting my things. 'I have to go. Can we continue this later?' I ask, looking at the confused faces.

'Abir, what happened?' Keerthi asks.

I need to call Amal and ask her why everyone is calling me. Anxiety roils around in my stomach.

'It's late, and my house is far from here.'

And how am I going to go back home? An Uber will be expensive and an auto will be hard to get at this hour. Why didn't I think of this before?

'I'll drop you home.' Sahil and Arsalan speak at the same moment.

If I weren't dying a little inside, I would have met Keerthi's gaze. We might have giggled together.

'I'll take an auto or Uber.'

'Don't be silly,' Keerthi says briskly. 'It will take forever for an auto to get here.'

'I have a motorbike and we'll reach sooner,' Sahil says, shutting the laptop and packing it away. 'Also, I know where you live.'

I'm wary of getting on a motorbike with him. If anyone who knows me spots me, it would be disastrous on many fronts.

'I think going back in a car would be better,' Arsalan says.

Keerthi is looking from Sahil to Arsalan with a glee I can recognize.

Hello, this is my life and not a sitcom.

'I just need to go now,' I mumble.

'I can drop you at a distance from the house,' Sahil suggests.

I turn to him.

'I can do that too.' Arsalan looks at me — really looks at me, as if he's conveying something to me with his eyes.

The Arsalan I know, the cocky scumbag who is always trying to take me down a peg or two, has disappeared completely. Or maybe I'd been mistaken about him all along.

'I think I'll go with Arsalan,' I tell Sahil. 'That would be . . .'

'Safer,' Arsalan says.

Sahil stiffens. 'I don't ride recklessly.'

'That's not what he meant,' I interrupt.

Really? I know what Arsalan meant?

'Fine,' Sahil says. He looks a little pissed.

And I think back to what Amal had said — that she thinks Sahil likes me. That had jolted me then, making me think of him in a new light.

This is like my dream. But I'm the dining table now.

'Let's go,' I tell Arsalan. 'Thank you for everything, Keerthi.'

'And we're meeting here after college tomorrow, right? Or how will this get done?' she asks.

I don't know. How I'm received back home today will decide everything. If my father finds out that I've come back home in a car with a boy, he might just disown me. And Ammi? I don't even want to think about that right now.

Sahil, Arsalan and I walk out of the villa. Sahil gives me a piercing look as he goes to get his motorbike. Arsalan and I walk over to the car.

I want to tell him to hurry, but I stop myself. He's doing me a favour. There's not much I can do except hope he can get me home soon.

As we drive off, I type out a message to Amal:

All okay at home?

Where are you?

On my way back

Abbu is asking where you are

I tell Arsalan where to drop me and then call Ammi.

'Where are you?' she asks sharply. 'Why didn't you answer?'

'I was at Keerthi's place. I told you I was going there. And my phone was on silent.'

'I don't like this, Abir,' Ammi says.

'I know, but it's for the project and . . .'

'I don't know if you should be doing that.'

'I've already registered for it,' I tell her quietly, wishing Arsalan wasn't listening to this conversation.

'So?'

'Ammi please. I'll come home and explain. You tell Abbu.'

I hang up. The silence in the car is heavy.

'So how long have you known this Sahil?' Arsalan asks suddenly.

I glance at him, a little bemused, a little thrill kicking about inside. *He's jealous? Why on earth would he be jealous?*

'He's my aunt's brother-in-law,' I explain. 'Thanks for dropping me, Arsalan.'

His mouth curves into a grimace-smile. 'No problem,' he says. 'I'll be more circumspect about the time from tomorrow.'

Tomorrow is something I'm a little wary about right now.

32

I stare up at the ceiling as I lie in bed. Sleep is not going to come easily.

Abbu had been livid when I walked into the house at seven thirty. I had to listen to him rage about how he was giving his daughters opportunities to make something for themselves, not go gallivanting around the city.

'My daughters go to school and college and come right back home. They don't go to anyone else's house. Who is this girl? Where does she live? How could you have allowed her to go?' Abbu asked, turning to Ammi.

Ammi had paled, but she couldn't get a word in edgewise.

Then I had to tell him that I had to go there tomorrow too.

'Are you serious? Why?'

'The competition is next month, and I need to finish working on it,' I mumbled.

'Why is this competition so important all of a sudden?' Abbu asked. 'Is it more important than your exams?'

I shook my head.

'Then? There's no need to waste your time on all this other stuff,' he said. 'Just focus on your studies, and pass your exams, and then we can think about your undergraduate degree and then marriage.'

Abbu's assumption that I would fall into line just because I was his daughter made me want to scream into the void.

'Abbu, I want to do my post-graduation. And then work for some time. I will not be ready for marriage any time soon,' I said.

Abbu stared at me as if I'd suddenly grown horns on my head. He dismissed me with a wave, the look of disbelief and disappointment so harsh on his face that it made my stomach curdle. I hated that I had so little control over my life.

Maybe the three of them—Sahil, Arsalan and Keerthi—could meet at her place and work on it, while I came back home like a good girl. The idea of other people building my app while I wasn't around made me feel like I'd swallowed a bunch of nails. If my pitch got selected and if the app did get made, then it wasn't just about helping my mother transform the way her business worked. It was also about getting myself a leg up into the next phase of my life.

Amal turns to me and nudges my elbow. 'Api, what are you going to do?' she asks in a small voice.

'About?'

'About your plans.'

'I'm not changing them.' I tell her firmly.

'But what will you do with Abbu?'

'I don't know, Amal. I can't change his mind with words. I'll have to change his mind with actions. I'm going to make sure that my app gets made. That should show him that I'm serious about all this. That I'm not studying because it's a checkmark to be made about my accomplishments. I'm studying to become someone, and I will.'

'I'm scared,' Amal says.

I turn to her and scoff. '*You're* scared?'

She nods. 'I don't like it when you get in trouble. And this looks like a lot of trouble.'

'I won't get into trouble,' I tell her.

'But if Sahil isn't coming here and you're not allowed to go to Keerthi's house so she can help you, how will you make it happen?'

I badly want to tell her the truth, but I stop myself. Amal is trustworthy, but she's a terrible keeper of secrets.

'We'll try and work on it in college,' I tell her.

We fall silent. The sounds around us magnify. The whirring of the ceiling fan, the little creaks around the house as Nani goes to the bathroom, the light pattering of footsteps as Abbu and Ammi go to the terrace.

I sit up and move closer to the window. If I position myself correctly and if they're standing on this side of the terrace, I can hear them speak sometimes.

'What are you doing?' Amal asks, eyes wide in the semi-darkness of the room.

'Sshh . . .'

I angle my head higher, as if that will help me make out their words better.

'. . . daughter . . .'

'. . . wants to do . . .'

'. . . but not right . . .'

'. . . marriage and the right . . .'

'. . . know what's right . . .'

Sighing, I fall back on the bed. They're most likely discussing my transgressions, and I hate that I have so little control over any of it.

'Api,' Amal whispers again.

'Hmm?'

'So, Sahil won't be coming home then?' she asks.

I turn to her and frown. 'You seem to be far too interested in his comings and goings,' I say accusingly.

She blinks, and her face becomes flushed. 'Shut up. I was thinking about how you two will spend time together if he doesn't come,' she says.

'I'm not interested in him that way.'

She gapes at me. 'Why?'

I giggle. 'If anything happened, don't you know who my mother-in-law will be?'

She winces. 'But . . . this isn't fair. *One* cute guy we know, and he's out of bounds.'

Everything was out of bounds, I think. *Cute guys, working on a plan, staying out late . . .*

And that's when the idea comes to me. If I can't go to Keerthi's place after college . . . they've left me with no choice but deception.

33

'**W**hat do you think?'

'I think it's a great idea!' Keerthi says. 'Why didn't I think of it?'

We are outside one of the buildings in college. I have been waiting for her to show up.

'So if you're sure, and if you're sure, aunty won't mind . . .'

'She won't!' Keerthi says, her eyes lighting up.

I know she wants to ask me about the car ride back with Arsalan last evening, but I'd ambushed her. The idea of bunking half the day from college so we can work in her house appeals to her. She, and even I, can't believe that the idea came from *me*.

'So I'll text Sahil and ask if he can make it?'

She nods. 'And yeah, Arsalan will take us home.'

'Do we have to?' I ask with a soft groan.

'Of course!' Keerthi says. 'He wants to be a part of this. How can you deny him that? Besides, he seems to know something about all this stuff as well. More than I know.'

I know my expression betrays my confused feelings because Keerthi puts her hand on mine. 'I know you worry a lot, Abir. But it's a part of who you are. I won't ask you not to worry and to pretend that everything is going to be fine. But think of this as an adventure.'

'What's the adventure?'

'All of it. Sneaking out of college, working on the app, spending time with Arsalan.'

'To what end?' I ask her, unable to stop myself.

She sighs. 'To no end but itself. This is all part of your college experience. Do you really want to finish college and then regret that you hadn't taken that one step in a different direction?'

I think of Ammi and how all her dreams had been ground to dust because of Nana. How can she not see that she's letting Abbu do the same thing to me? I won't let it happen. I know he loves me. I can only hope that his love for me transcends his notion of how things should happen in my life.

'Okay, so we bunk during lunch,' I tell her.

She nods. 'Oh my god, this is such fun!'

'Won't your mother be angry?' I ask, worried that her mother might think I'm a bad influence on her.

'Dude, if only you knew the kind of things she got up to when she was in college. And we're not bunking classes to party.'

I nod. 'Okay.'

'And here comes Arsalan. You tell him while I call Ma,' she says, leaving me alone with him, a move that has now become as predictable as it is exasperating. I look at her with affection as she rushes off, her phone to her ear, her ponytail bobbing.

'Hey! All good?' Arsalan asks, his eyes tracking my face in a way I'd never noticed before. It's like he's trying to read my micro-expressions.

'Yeah, we have a slight hitch, though.'

'What happened?'

I don't know how much he'd understand if I told him about my parents being angry with me. Keerthi didn't get it at all. For my parents, going to anyone's house to hang out was a concept that was unheard of. 'Um, are you still interested in the project?'

A hurt look crosses his face for a bare second before his face turns blank. 'I don't know what you want me to prove to you, Abir, but . . .' he begins in a low voice.

Without thinking, I put my hand on his elbow. Both of us freeze. He looks at my hand pointedly, and I pull it away, because my skin feels prickly where I touched him.

'I didn't mean it like that. I won't be able to go to Keerthi's place after college, so I suggested we bunk college after lunch and go there. We can work on the app, and I can reach home at the time I usually do.'

His face splits into a slow smile. 'Devious.'

'Not really. Desperate times call for desperate measures.'

'Of course, I'm in,' he says, stepping forward.

I step back, but miss placing my foot on the ground, and immediately he clutches my elbow and steadies me.

We enter the classroom without another word. We sit in our usual places. Keerthi comes in and sits with me.

I send a hurried text to Sahil. I feel bad asking him to miss his classes, but what else can we do? He responds back with a thumbs-up emoji.

As the third hour of class starts, my stomach churns. We're going to have to leave college as soon as the lunch bell rings.

'Why can't we just find a coffee shop nearby to do this?' I ask Keerthi in a whisper.

She shrugs. 'What if your dad finds out that you're sitting in a coffee shop with two hot guys instead of studying in college?'

Girls from families like mine can neither be seen nor heard. We are just a vague entity that people remember whenever talk of proposals started.

As the minutes tick by, my anxiety goes up. *Is what I'm doing all right?* I'm not doing anything immoral or illegal and that's the only issue my parents should have. But I know how they are.

'Let's go,' I whisper the moment the bell rings.

I spot Arsalan walking down the stairs too, with Luke. I don't mind Luke, but I don't want him to be in the team. I find his presence too disruptive.

Luke slaps Arsalan on the back and turns in the direction of the canteen. Arsalan smirks at the evident relief on my face.

'There's just one problem,' Arsalan says as he opens the front passenger door for me.

'What?'

'How are we going to explain our attendance?' he asks.

'To whom?'

He sits in the driver's seat as Keerthi gets in the back. 'To our parents. That's whom they'll call when they find our attendance is low. They make a big fuss when it's time to give us hall tickets for the final exams.'

My stomach hurts. I wonder if I am getting an ulcer. 'Let's handle one problem at a time.'

He looks at me with concern. 'You okay?'

I am anything but okay. But this conundrum will drive me crazy. 'I don't know. I just want to get this app done. And soon.'

He gives me another long look. 'We'll get it done soon, Abir,' he says in a reassuring tone.

'Yeah, we better. Not all of us have cool parents like Keerthi,' I remark.

'Yeah, my parents are chill. What about your parents, Arsalan?' Keerthi asks.

He grimaces. 'They are anything but chill.' His gaze finds mine. He only looks away when he begins to drive.

34

'You look tired,' Nani says.

'Yes, college has been quite tough,' I respond.

A week of this dual life has exhausted me. Lying gets easier as you keep doing it but it still takes energy. There's a load of work that I need to catch up on from all the missed classes. I just want to get all of this done and not get into trouble with my parents.

The good thing is that one week of consistent work has ensured that we have the bare bones of the app in place. Of course, it's still laughably not ready. But a lot has happened. We need to test it. We need to practise the pitching part as well.

The weekend is here. We decided to pick it back up on Monday.

The reprieve is good in more ways than one.

I don't know what to do about these strange new feelings that have popped up. I can't recall why I used to be so annoyed by Arsalan. I hadn't realized how easily he makes people laugh. He mimics people and says the funniest things with a deadpan expression. His impression of Mr Jairaj, our maths teacher, had everyone, including Keerthi's mother, in splits.

Arsalan and Sahil seem to have developed a polite understanding, but things are still a little prickly, much to Keerthi's amusement. Navigating between them is one of the reasons for my exhaustion. Also, it's not funny how they try to one-up each other when it comes to different sections of the code.

Keerthi thinks it is the modern software equivalent of tech bros trying to woo a woman by writing a code that will appeal to her. I've told her what I think of that idea.

Arsalan offers to drop me home every day, but I refuse each time. I've found a bus stop near Keerthi's house, and I take the bus back. Once or twice, Sahil has offered to drop me off at the bus stop, and I've agreed because it seems churlish to keep saying no.

According to Keerthi, Arsalan's expression has been *priceless* each time I get behind Sahil on the motorbike. I don't know what she means.

My phone buzzes. It's a text from Keerthi.

I miss the boy drama!

I don't and I want this to b done soon

I wonder wht Arsalan is doing nw. Do u follow him on social?

No, and I don't want to. After that horrifying reel about the two of us, I haven't looked much at Instagram.

No. No time. I'll see you on Monday

I walk to my room where Amal is sitting in her corner of the bed, studying. The sight is comforting. I pull out my notebooks and start completing all the notes I've missed this past week. I've had to grovel and beg the front benchers to send me their notes, and they agreed reluctantly.

The day stretches out before me, filled with work and studies, but the usual rush I feel isn't quite there. It's like there's something missing. *That's ridiculous, right?*

Amal and I work in companionable silence. After a while, she looks up and frowns. 'How come you have so much work to do?'

I shrug. 'II PUC isn't a joke.'

She rolls her eyes but goes back to work.

We venture out when Ammi calls us to help hang out the washed clothes on the terrace. Pushing my phone into the pocket of my salwar, I go and pick up the bucket. Amal comes too.

Ammi looks at both of us. That quivering smile on her face makes me want to hug her and scream at her at the same time. Parental love is exasperating.

As Amal and I hang the clothes, I catch my sister casting strange glances at me.

'What is it?' I ask her finally.

'Something has changed,' she says.

'What?'

'About you. You've become looser.'

'I'm sorry, what?' I ask, a little horrified. *What does she even mean?*

'You've always walk with this tight set to your shoulders. And your spine is stiff. But that intensity has lowered a bit.'

I scan her face, not sure if she's joking. She's serious.

'So you're saying I was uptight, but I'm not any longer?'

She nods. 'It's one of the things that's changed. Your face is also a little extra glow-y. Have you started some new skincare regimen that you haven't told me about?'

I open my mouth to protest, but I stop. 'Yeah. It's not a big deal.'

'It is a big deal, Api! Tell me what you're doing! I want skin like yours too!' she says, her eyes wide.

'First, let's go down. The sun is too hot.'

'And no sunscreen,' she wails, hurrying downstairs. I'm glad for a moment that our mutual obsession over skincare has won over her curiosity.

My phone buzzes. I look down at the phone to see Keerthi has just set up a WhatsApp group called 'The Henna Start-up', and it has me, Arsalan, Sahil and herself. The logo of the group is an illustration of a girl bent over a palm with a mehendi cone in her hand. It has a very comic book feel to it, but it hits the right spots. My heart expands with love and gratitude for this quirky friend of mine.

Without exiting the group to text her separately, I send a message.

Have I told you how much I love you?

35

Before I can hit delete for everyone, the ticks turn blue, which means everyone in the group has seen it.

Thankfully, Keerthi saves my ass.

Aww, I love u 2 boo!

I don't know why she set up the group, but it feels strangely good, like we're all connected to each other. I call Keerthi.

'Hello!' she says in a low drawl.

'Hey!'

'That was so cool of you. *Have I told you how much I love you?*'

I groan. 'Shut up.'

'No, I get it. They're both hot, so why choose?' she giggles.

'Eww,' I snap at her.

I walk into my room. Amal looks up at me. She's standing near the tiny dressing table we share and trying to figure out if I've recently bought any new products.

'Okay fine. Far be it from me to try and push something into happening,' Keerthi whines in my ear.

'Nothing is going to happen!' I tell her furiously. Amal gives me a curious look.

'But don't you just wish it would?' Keerthi insists.

'That's not how this works,' I whisper. 'I'll see you on Monday.' Before she can protest, I end the call.

'Who was that?' Amal asks.

'Keerthi,' I tell her.

'So, how's the app going? Is it still happening?'

I nod.

'You've been really quiet all these days.'

'I've just been busy, Amal. I don't trouble you when you have big projects to submit, right?'

She looks hurt, and I feel terrible.

'I didn't mean it like that,' I tell her weakly.

She shrugs. 'Nida Phuppu and Samreen Khala are both coming over this afternoon,' she says.

I perk up immediately. 'Oh, are they coming here to spend the evening?' I ask.

She shakes her head. 'No, Ammi's got another big order, and she needs help.'

'She needs both of them?'

'Yeah. They'll leave once Abbu goes to the shop after lunch.'

I sit down on the bed, wondering when Abbu will realize that Ammi hides whatever she's doing just to pander to his ego. *Why are men's egos so big anyway?*

Samreen Khala and Nida Phuppu arrive after lunch. They have no time to chat. They're busy checking their cones and if they have all the patterns. I look at them, and realize that if we manage to win the pitch, we would have to consider marketing as well. Obviously, the app has to scale up the existing situation. There's no point in making an app just for my mother and aunts. Ammi will have to train new people.

'What's the event?' I ask.

'It's a sangeet, and they want henna for all the women.'

Ammi shoots me a look. 'We're taking an advance and we're charging them properly.'

'Maybe you can ask them if they'd be interested if there was an app for this,' I suggest.

Samreen Khala looks at me and frowns. 'So, you're doing it? The henna app?'

I nod quickly.

'How? You said you'd need Sahil's help,' Samreen Khala says.

Ammi gives her a sharp look. 'Yes, he came home once, but that didn't work out. So she's doing it with her friend's help in college.'

I try not to wince. *Lies, lies, lies.*

Samreen Khala gives me a strange look. 'I see. I want to talk to you when you have time, Abir,' she says.

What? Why?

'Yeah, sure,' I say. I hope that it's late by the time they return, so there is no time to talk. I will most likely crumble under Samreen Khala's interrogation. She is like a friend, but I don't want to get into trouble with her.

If Ammi or she were to know that I spent the past week working on this app with two boys, they'd die of mortification. For them, the end is not important, but the means to it would be everything. I might as well say goodbye to talking to Ammi and Samreen Khala ever again.

36

'We'll knock it out of the park during the pitch,' Arsalan assures me when I look at our app doubtfully.

'It's the best we can do for now,' Sahil echoes my thoughts.

The app is not bad, I have to admit. The latest version of it is on Keerthi's laptop. Hers is sleek and fast and way better than mine. So thankfully, I don't have to worry about taking mine to college.

We've tested the prototype repeatedly, and so far, everything seems to work as it's meant to. The app opens to a beautiful henna background that fades away to show the interface. It's still a little basic, but hopefully the pitch will compensate for the bells and whistles.

It has taken ten days of missed classes, and finally we are ready. Sort of. I really hope my attendance percentage isn't too low to require my parents' intervention. I'd heard that some colleges sent messages to parents that their children had missed a class. Post-pandemic, that hasn't resumed at our college, and I'm just thankful.

'This was good fun. Thank you for everything,' Arsalan tells Sahil, extending his hand. Sahil looks at his hand, as if it's a snake, but he takes it. Keerthi nudges me rather obviously and I glare at her.

Sahil glances over at me. 'I can drop you off today,' he says, indicating that we should leave.

That seems a little proprietary, and I don't like his tone. But I smile at him and shake my head. 'I have something to discuss with Keerthi. I'll head to the bus stop in a bit.'

He looks at me, as if unsure to leave me with Keerthi and Arsalan. I have to stop myself from rolling my eyes.

'It looks like it's going to rain,' he says, glancing out of the window.

The sky *has* turned dark. Bangalore has been unreasonably hot the past few days, and whenever that happens, it almost always rains to cool off a bit.

'I'll drop her at the bus stop in the car,' Arsalan says.

Sahil's nostrils flare a little, but he nods and turns around to leave. I feel a smidgen of unease. I've enjoyed working with him, and I feel like he deserves better.

'Sahil,' I call out when he's nearly at the door. He turns around.

I walk up to him, aware of Arsalan's gaze and Keerthi's. She's probably munching on virtual popcorn at this drama playing out.

'Yeah?'

I walk up to him. He's really good looking in a broody sort of way, but his proximity does nothing to me. Zilch.

'Thank you for everything. I don't know how we could have done this without you.'

He nods, his gaze on my face almost as if he's searching for something there.

'If we get selected and get some funding, you can be sure that you're getting your share.'

His expression turns blank, and there's a flash of disappointment. 'Yeah, whatever,' he says and leaves.

I come back to sit on the sofa. Arsalan is sprawled on another. I have to drag my eyes away from his lean body, his long legs and the way he just seems to make himself so comfortable in every space.

'I think we should start practising the pitch,' he says.

'You two should do it,' Keerthi says.

I sigh and look at her. 'Why? Why not you and me?'

'A boy and a girl. Always looks good,' she says teasingly. 'I mean, think of the symmetry! And you two look good together.'

There's an awkward silence. I don't know where to look. To say this in front of Arsalan! I could clobber her.

'I'm happy to do the pitch with Abir,' Arsalan says, ignoring her words. 'Although, I think she can rock it alone. Whoever else is there will just be offering support.'

'I'll take all the support I can,' I say. I still can't bring myself to look at him.

There's a flash of lightning, and thunder rumbles in the distance. I can smell rain in the air. Sahil was right.

'That's my cue to leave,' I tell them, hoping I can make it to the bus stop before it begins to rain. I collect my things, and over Arsalan and Keerthi's protests, I leave.

The bus stop isn't too far but before I can reach it, a jagged bolt of lightning crosses the sky. It's feels like evening already. The sky is dark, and fat raindrops start falling on my head like they're in a hurry to drench me.

'Shit,' I mutter under my breath.

By the time I reach the bus stop, it's a full-fledged downpour.

My abaya is soaked through and sticking to me uncomfortably. I hold my bag close to my body and shiver a little. There's no one else at the bus stop, and it's a little scary. This stretch of road seems isolated in the rain. In the distance, there's a tiny shack, and I can make out a few blurry figures.

Then a car comes down the road. I know immediately that it's Arsalan's.

Arsalan stops and rolls down his window. 'Get inside the car, Abir!'

I jump in quickly so that the rain doesn't get inside.

'Why did you leave in such a hurry?' he asks as he shifts gears and starts driving.

'I thought I'd get the bus, and I didn't think the rain would start so soon,' I tell him.

The wipers are moving over the windshield rhythmically. I'm a bit mortified at getting his upholstery wet. But he doesn't seem to care.

When the downpour doesn't relent, he stops the car in a lane.

'What are you doing?' I ask him.

'We have to wait this out. I can't see a thing,' he says.

The pattering of rain on the car roof is deafening, emphasizing the silence inside the car. The contrasts create an intimate atmosphere that has me looking anywhere but him.

My heart is racing. When I finally turn to him, he is looking at me too.

37

The moment stretches between us. The look in his eyes deepens, and my body heats up even though I'm drenched.

I want to say something. But I've forgotten how to speak.

It feels as if he's aware of the power of words. If he says anything, it might shatter this fragile, intense moment.

He startles me by picking up my hand.

I've touched him before. When I fell into his arms that day, or when he put those keys in my hands, but none of those moments had been deliberate. This is different.

The texture of his skin is rough, so different from mine. I can feel his calluses press into the soft flesh of my palms. A warm, tingling feeling emerges from some indescribable point in my body and grows until it encompasses me fully.

His thumb moves over the soft, fleshy base of my thumb. It's as if I've been stripped of my skin, and every nerve ending is exposed.

I look up at him. His gaze is darker than ever. When I lick my dry lips, his eyes fall to them, and then they're back up at my eyes.

'I like you, Abir,' he says in a low voice.

I should pull my hand away from his. *This isn't right.*

So what if I can't stop thinking about him? I don't even like him, right? He and I never got along.

He and I are nothing alike.

He's rich, I'm lower middle class. He's irreverent and charming and annoying. I'm studious and nerdy and love plans. He won't know a plan if it hits him on the head. It's his privilege that makes him so chilled out. He makes friends wherever he goes—even Keerthi's watchman is now his buddy. I cannot be bothered to learn anyone's name because I think it will ruin my focus.

Yet, when Arsalan runs his thumb slowly along the length of mine, my body reacts wildly to his touch.

He's nothing like the guy I thought he was.

'I like you too,' I tell him softly.

My heart is pounding so loudly that I'm sure people in the next lane can hear it over the rain.

He lifts his other hand to trace my cheek with his thumb. The look of surprise on his face is gratifying. 'You have incredible skin,' he murmurs.

'I know,' I tell him, feeling a little smug.

But that evaporates when his thumb moves to my lip.

Don't. Don't do this.

I pull his hand away from my lips. His hand trembles.

Our faces come closer, closer and closer. I know that what's going to happen will change everything. I'm free-falling.

Our lips touch, hesitantly at first. His are firm and soft and then with a small groan, he deepens the kiss, holding my head between his hands, angling his own.

For all my knowledge, for all my awareness, I feel like I've been living a half-life until this moment.

I'm kissing Arsalan Khan.

The thought is so ridiculous that it jars me out of the moment. I break away. His gaze moves between my lips and my eyes. I know he wants to kiss me again, but I sit back in the seat, trembling a little.

'Abir, say something, dammit,' he mutters.

'I want to go home,' I tell him quietly.

'And what happened . . . this . . .'

What does a kiss mean to someone like Arsalan? He had kissed Luke to make a point to us. He had probably kissed dozens of girls because he certainly seemed to know what he was doing.

I'd just be one more notch in his belt if I behaved like the kiss meant more than it did.

It meant way more.

'It was just a kiss,' I tell him with a forced smile. 'It doesn't have to mean anything more.'

His eyes rove over my face. 'Are you serious?' he asks finally.

'It was a moment of madness,' I tell him. 'So embarrassing. I think I can get the bus if I leave now.' I make to open the door when he stops me.

'Stop it, Abir,' he says, his breath shuddering out. 'I'll drop you.'

He drops me off at the corner near my house. I get down with a quick thank you and walk away without looking back.

38

When I walk into the house, Samreen Khala is sitting on the sofa, talking to Ammi.

I haven't got around to talking to Samreen Khala since the time she said we should talk. There's a glow on Ammi's face, and it lightens my heart. It's odd how my happiness is connected to Ammi's. I feel I can do anything when Ammi is happy.

The kiss.

I can't think of it right now. I need to process this in my room, preferably alone.

Ammi frowns. 'Abir, why are you wet, beta?'

Though my abaya has dried mostly, I'm still damp in patches. 'I got caught in the rain at the bus stop,' I tell her.

Samreen Khala eyes me curiously. *Why is she here? If they're going for a job, why are they sitting here doing gupshup?*

'Okay, change and come soon.' Ammi looks like she wants to say more, but Samreen Khala puts her hand on Ammi's. My unease increases.

I go to my room and quickly don dry clothes from my cupboard.

Arsalan's face swims before me.

My phone pings. *Is it him? What will I tell him?*

It's Keerthi who wants to know if I reached home safely and if Arsalan found me at the bus stop.

Yes.

I put the phone face down and sit down on my bed, holding my head in my hands. As a first kiss, it was . . . I don't have the vocabulary to process this just yet. I don't know what to do with it. *Why did I let it happen?*

I think back to those surreal moments inside his car, filled with the scent of his cologne and the dark intensity of his eyes and the confident way his lips had moved over mine. I touch my lips with the tips of my fingers, and something warm unfurls in my belly.

Me. Abir Maqsood. In trouble over a boy.

There's a knock on the door. I open it, expecting Amal.

Samreen Khala walks inside. She looks at me, and I try my best to keep my expression neutral.

'What's going on, Abir?' she asks me gently.

Her words undo something in my heart. I sit on the edge of the bed and start sobbing quietly. I'm an idiot. Other girls would not be overthinking the hell out of that kiss.

Why am I not like them?

Samreen Khala puts her hand on my shoulder. I turn to her, and she hugs me.

'Abir, Abir,' she says softly. 'It's okay, beta. I know.'

I go still. *What?*

'I know all this can be a bit overwhelming at first.'

'What?' I ask her, confused.

'Love,' she says.

'What?' This time, I'm shocked.

'Listen, don't worry. We won't tell anyone. We'll do this the regular way. For now, we'll just do a small ceremony limited to our houses, and then when you finish college . . .'

'What are you talking about?'

'Your marriage to Sahil,' she says, her smile growing wide.

No. No. What does she mean by my marriage?

'What are you talking about?' I ask her in a horrified whisper. I seem to be repeating the same words over and over again.

'Sahil told me everything,' she says.

My heart stops. 'What did he say?'

'That you have been taking his help all these days for your app. He really likes you, Abir. He came and told me that he would like to get engaged to you. Once you both finish studying, you can get married.'

I cover my mouth in shock.

Samreen Khala misinterprets it. 'This is the best news I've heard in a long time. Just imagine! You'll be my *devrani*!' She nudges me playfully. 'But our relationship won't change at all. I'll still be your aunt. You better not start calling me bhabhi.'

I want to tell her to stop talking. That this is all a horrendous mistake.

Before I can say anything, Ammi is at the door. Now her expression makes sense to me.

Her mouth is trembling a little. 'I can't imagine a better proposal for you, my darling Abir.' She bursts into tears.

'Arrey, Apa! Stop crying!' Samreen Khala chides her. 'Shush. Don't be silly. It's going to be fine. We're all going to be so happy together.'

Ammi walks inside the room and hugs me hard.

I move away from her and take a shaky breath. 'Ammi, I already told you I don't plan to get married even after I finish college. I want to do a post-graduate programme and then work.'

Samreen Khala smiles at me beatifically. 'Of course, you can do it after your marriage too. Sahil will be the most supportive husband you can ever find.'

And that's it.

They both turn to each other and start making all kinds of plans. My head feels like it's on fire. I watch them both in horror as they decide how they will package this news to the world.

'There will be no question about it being a love marriage,' Samreen Khala says firmly. 'No one needs to know that Sahil spoke to me about it and said that he likes her.'

Ammi covers her cheeks in embarrassment, as if Sahil had proposed to her. 'And Abir's father?'

'My husband is going to talk to him today. This *baat* will be *pakki aaj*.' She hugs me tightly.

She might as well have plunged a dagger into my chest.

39

I'm sick

What happnd?

Got wet in the rain and caught a cold

I'll come c u?

No I'll b fine

UR comng 2moro rt?

Ya

I push the phone deep under my pillow.

Things went from surreal to dystopian in the span of half an hour last night. Several times, I opened my mouth to say something — I don't quite know what — to Ammi or Samreen Khala, but they were so caught up in their fantasy that they just talked over me.

Amal was shocked but also delighted.

'I *told* you he likes you,' she crowed to me when we were sent to our room like errant children so the adults could talk and make decisions about my life, once

Abbu and Sadiq Uncle came home. Ammi was running around as though royalty had landed at our door. She insisted I stay inside my room while my brother-in-law-to-be was outside.

Once more, I was not telling my sister anything. But what could I tell her? That I liked someone else? That I'd *kissed* him?

Nani ambled inside my room and sat on the bed. She smiled at me. 'They're talking about wedding dates,' she said.

What the hell?

Seeing the expression on my face, Nani quickly amended. 'Which year, I meant. Wedding year. Not date.'

Amal went out to help Ammi in the kitchen.

Nani seemed to sense that something was wrong. 'Look, beta. This is a wonderful opportunity. We all like Sahil. They'll just fix your wedding once you finish your studies. It solves so many problems.'

What problems?

Nani touched my cheek. Her eyes glowed. 'You are very lucky. If someone has seen you somewhere and sent a proposal, you can never be sure what sort of people they will be like. But we know Samreen's in-laws. We know Sahil. We know everyone there. It will be like going from one home to another. Another familiar house. Not a stranger's.'

Her words are no comfort to me. *What about all my plans? What about all the things I wanted to do for the family? How could all my ambitions have been swept away because of a proposal?*

How could Sahil do this to me?

I considered him a friend. He had helped me tremendously. How could he assume that I wanted to get engaged to him? I'm too young for this!

Not young enough to kiss Arsalan, a sly voice erupted in my head.

Sahil could have at least warned me, or for the love of god, he could have asked me what I felt. I have a good mind to call him up and yell at him, but not right now.

This morning, I told Ammi I was feeling feverish, and I didn't go to college. My life was destroyed. And it was all because of a guy who was not even the guy I liked.

I doze on and off.

Ammi walks in, her face lit up. Since last night, she has been unable to stop smiling. Apparently, she'd prayed for some miracle like this. And now that this miracle has taken place, she's floating on air. She's all light and air and hope.

'Abir beta, come and eat. I have some firni for you,' she says.

'No thanks,' I mumble. I don't want to leave this bed. Also, that was the firni she made for Sadiq Uncle last night.

'Are you okay? Do we need to go to the doctor?'

I feel like death.

This is the twenty-first century. This can't be happening, seriously.

'No, I'll be fine.' I tell her. I need her to leave.

The problem is that once I shut my eyes, I see Arsalan, sitting in the car, leaning close to me.

My phone rings.

I pull it warily out from under the pillow. I'm shocked to see that it's a call from Arsalan. I can't talk to him.

I silence the ringer and watch his name light up on my screen. Even his name makes my heart do somersaults.

When the call stops, my phone buzzes with a message.

R u ok?

I am anything but okay, but telling him that might make him call me again. Or worse, what if he decides to come home to see me? Nah, he wouldn't, I think nervously. But obviously, these guys have cow dung instead of brains. So, who knows?

Say smthg

I already said what I needed to yesterday, but my heart still yearns for him, for the way he laughs, for the way that slow smile grows on his face . . .

I am so screwed.

40

'Can we meet?'

'I thought you weren't well,' Keerthi sounds surprised when she hears my voice over the phone.

I need to speak to her. I need to talk to someone or I will quite possibly explode.

'I'm okay now. Let's meet somewhere we can talk, please.'

She makes a 'hmm' sound. 'Sure. You tell me where you want to meet.'

I glance at the clock in my bedroom. 'I'll meet you in the coffee shop near college?'

'You want to come so far?' she asks, surprised.

'Yes. I'll see you there in half an hour.'

Ammi is surprised to see me leave. 'But you had fever and all that?'

'Ammi, I need to meet Keerthi about the pitch,' I tell her, my face heating a little. 'It's happening in a couple of weeks, and we need to practice.'

'But . . .'

'I'll be back soon.' I leave before she can come up with reasons why I shouldn't go out.

I don't wait for a bus. I get into an auto, and half an hour later, I am inside the bustling coffee shop.

God, I missed coffee shops during the pandemic — the sound of the coffee bean grinders, the ambient music, the chatter of people floating everywhere. I hadn't been to many because, before COVID, I was in Grade IX. And the prices made my heart lurch. But I liked the idea of them. Being in a coffee shop makes me feel like I am a part of a vibrant city like Bangalore, living a life and not just existing.

Keerthi's not here yet. I find an empty table for us. I tell the hovering waiter that we will order when my friend arrives.

I had finally replied to Arsalan's message, telling him I was all right. But I know he would read more into my absence because of what happened last evening.

Keerthi walks in, looking cooler and fresher than I ever would at the end of a college day. 'Hey! What happened? You weren't well, and now you're well?'

I look into her concerned eyes. 'Arsalan and I kissed.'

Her eyes grow wide, and she opens her mouth to shriek.

'And Sahil talked to my aunt, and she came over last night with a proposal for marriage.'

'What?'

I tell her everything. She's stunned. We order two lattes, and I keep talking, telling her all the things that happened since I left her home. When I'm done, she draws in a breath and then blows it out in a whoosh.

'My god. What *is* this drama?'

'My life,' I tell her bitterly.

'Okay, before we do anything to fix this fiasco—' she says.

I feel momentarily heartened. I know she holds no sway with my parents, but I still feel better because she said 'we'.

'You need to tell me everything about that kiss,' she hisses, leaning forward.

'No. Don't make me,' I groan, covering my face.

'Abir,' she says in an awe-struck voice. 'You have got it bad, girl.'

I know. 'I told him it was no big deal.'

'Wait up. You said what?' she asks in a hushed whisper.

'What was I supposed to say?' I whisper back. 'He's probably kissed hundreds of girls. Dozens at least.'

Keerthi rolls her eyes. 'Who cares about that? And what does it have to do with the two of you?'

'You know how I am. I'm a stick in the mud. I like things done a certain way. I have plans for my life. And they don't involve . . .' I trail off.

'He kept looking at the door, waiting for you to walk inside the classroom,' Keerthi says. 'When you didn't show up after the first hour, he asked me where you were. I told him you weren't well. He looked quite . . .' she taps her lips thoughtfully. 'Upset? No. Too small a word. Devastated? No. Too big. Something in between.' She waves her hand to indicate the middle. 'He left the classroom before the next teacher could come in. I wondered what could have happened, but of course, I'd never have even *dreamt* about any of this.'

That had been when he called me. And sent me those messages.

'So, what did he do after that?' I ask her, needing to know more.

She shrugs. 'I don't know.'

41

It's amazing how much better I feel after talking to Keerthi. I know she has no clue about my world, and none of the ideas she's outlining will work. Still, it feels good to see the plans she has scribbled on a paper napkin.

All of them are rubbish.

- *Kidnap Sahil* (How will that help?)

- *Kidnap Arsalan* (Why though? Just for fun, she says.)

- *Tell parents about Arsalan* (They'll kill me.)

- *Tell Sahil about Arsalan* (I've got a feeling he knows and he must have done this to pre-empt anything from happening from that end.)

- *Tell Samreen Khala about Arsalan* (This is the only viable option. But I cannot imagine having this conversation with her or any other member of my family.)

'Why do we need to tell anyone about him?' I ask her after a while. Our coffees are long over. The waiter has walked past a couple of times, trying to see if we're going to leave.

She shrugs. 'Because your ambition alone is not enough for people to stop and listen to you?'

Last night, at dinner, Abbu had been cautiously approving of Sahil. He said that if this wedding got fixed, it would solve a lot of problems. *What problems was he referring to? Why did people think I was a problem?*

When he saw my expression, he elaborated. 'It would give a message to the world that we have already considered your future and have made the decision that is best for you.'

How was it the best for me? In which world? A world where I was only a daughter and not a person in my own right? A world where I was not expected to have any ambitions and dreams of my own but support the men in my life?

I refuse to accept that.

Last night, I kept quiet because I couldn't tell Abbu outright that I refused this proposal. I needed to sort out a plan. And I need to talk to Sahil.

'Your life is like one of those Pakistani dramas my mom watches,' Keerthi says.

'Your mom watches them so she can drool over Fawad Khan,' I tell her, rolling my eyes.

'True. But this level of drama is . . .'

'Something that I hate,' I tell her vehemently. 'I want a normal life. I want to finish my education without having a fiancé who is ready to marry me the moment I walk out of my last exam. I want to be able to think about what's coming next in my life without having to worry about what potential in-laws will say.'

Keerthi looks at me, her eyes wide. 'I never thought about any of this.'

'And you don't need to either,' I tell her.

'Okay, first things first. We are going to ask Sahil to come and meet you. Then I'll try my best not to hit him over the head with something,' she says, enumerating the points on her fingers.

'And then?'

'Then, let him talk to his folks, and you talk to your parents. Not about Arsalan, but about your life plans. Tell them you're serious about it.'

I've told them many times. They just keep thinking of it as white noise coming out of my mouth. I don't know how to make them listen.

'And then,' she leans forward.

'And then?' I ask her, confused.

'And then we tackle Arsalan.'

42

Amal looks at me as we leave the house the following morning to get the bus.

'You don't look as happy as I thought you'd be,' she says.

I stay quiet in Mahim Chacha's auto. She keeps looking at me.

On the bus, I get a window seat. I look outside, trying to steady my nerves. A lot is going to happen today.

Amal puts her hand on mine. 'Api, you *are* happy, right?'

'You know, no one else has asked me that,' I tell her in a low voice. I don't feel like listening to music because my head is already blaring with thoughts.

'But why aren't you happy?' she asks, looking troubled. 'I thought you liked Sahil and . . .'

'I'm not ready for this,' I tell her. 'I don't want to think about all this when my exams are coming up, when I have to get my pitch ready. I have a lot on my mind.'

She looks hurt. There is one thing that I need to tell her, though. 'You always said that you thought he liked me.'

She nods, her teeth worrying her lower lip.

'I never said that I liked him back.'

We don't talk after that. As she gets down at her stop, she turns to me. 'I just want you to be happy, okay?'

I nod solemnly, but I don't know how I'm going to be happy.

When I reach college, it feels like I haven't seen Arsalan in months. It's just been a little over a day since we met. *Since we kissed.* I push the thought away.

As I walk into class, my eyes do a quick sweep, but he's not there. Disappointment seeps into me. I sit at my usual spot and soon Keerthi joins me.

We've made plans for today. The first thing is talking to Sahil. He started this mess. He'd better end it.

I'm not able to concentrate. Keerthi knows this and has been taking notes diligently with many dejected sighs. In the middle of all my stress, this makes me smile.

I had texted Sahil and asked him to meet me in college during lunch. At the appointed time, we wait near the gates.

When we spot him riding his motorbike inside the campus, Keerthi waves at him. He stops, parks the bike, and then walks over to us, helmet in hand.

I want to slap him.

'Hi,' he says, looking at me and ignoring Keerthi.

'Why did you do it?' I ask him.

He stares at me for long moments. 'I thought we liked each other,' he says finally.

'I'm not ready for any of this,' I tell him. I don't have the courage to say an outright no, and that bothers me.

'So, we're not doing anything right now. This is just like . . .'

'You're booking me. Right?' I ask, fury flashing in my eyes.

He puts his hands up in a conciliatory gesture. 'I know how things can snowball in a girl's life, Abir,' he says, stepping closer to me.

I take a step back, aware that there are curious glances directed our way. 'Meaning?'

'If someone sent a proposal for you, and your parents liked it, they'll go ahead and say yes,' he says. 'I thought if I did this, then you could focus on your studies without having to worry about anyone coming after you with a proposal.'

'Unless that anyone is you,' Keerthi pipes in.

He shoots her an irritated look. 'So, what if I did? I'm better than any of the random rishtas that can come her way. I won't pressure her for marriage, and we'll only get married once Abir is ready.'

My face is like a lobster—shiny and red. I decide it is time to tell Sahil in unvarnished words that I did not *like* him and that I had no intentions of marrying him at any point.

But just then, a voice behind me asks. 'Who's getting married?'

I turn. Arsalan is looking at the three of us, puzzled.

Now he comes to college?

And in the midst of my anger and distress, one part of my brain notices that he is wearing a white shirt with sleeves rolled up to his elbows and jeans. If Arsalan in a black pathani is kryptonite, this look is also pretty lethal.

Wait. What had he asked?

Sahil reaches out and picks up my hand. 'Abir and I are getting married,' he says.

The hell we are. I pull my hand away, but Sahil is standing way too close.

'Oh, I see,' Arsalan says, his voice steely. 'Abir is not even eighteen. It's illegal to get married. Married!' he scoffs.

'Somebody get me popcorn,' Keerthi whispers.

I glare at her as Sahil says, 'We're not marrying *now*.' Then I turn my glare on him.

Arsalan looks at me searchingly.

I shake my head. 'I'm not marrying you, Sahil. Not now, not ever.'

Sahil looks at me, confused. 'But . . .'

'I never told you to do what you did,' I tell him. 'It was just wrong. You should have talked to me . . .'

'What did he do?' Arsalan asks in a low voice.

'He sent her a proposal,' Keerthi says.

'And her family agreed,' Sahil says smugly.

There is panic on Arsalan's face, mixed with disbelief and even hurt.

'My family agreed. But I didn't,' I say because it is important he knows.

Sahil looks at me impatiently. 'Why didn't you say anything when the proposal came?' he asks.

'Because everyone ambushed me!' I tell him. 'You made this mess. Go fix it, Sahil.'

He looks at the three of us in turn, and then he shakes his head. 'No,' he says, and walks away.

43

'Should I have sent a proposal too?'

Keerthi and I turn to Arsalan.

'Quit joking, Arsalan,' Keerthi says.

The look on his face is utterly serious. I gulp, not sure why the idea of him sending a proposal is shocking, infuriating, but also . . . exciting.

'I'm serious,' he says.

'Why?'

'Let's find an empty classroom to hash this out,' Arsalan says, not looking away from me.

'There's nothing to hash out. Nothing to talk about. I am not getting married to anyone,' I announce. I just want a normal, no-drama life. But apparently, that's too much to ask for.

Arsalan steps forward as if to convince me, but I put my hand out to stop him. 'Not now, Arsalan. Please. Don't even joke about this.'

'I'm not joking.'

'Then it's even worse!' I snap out at him. 'How can you say such a thing? Why would you even want to do this?'

'Guys . . .' Keerthi looks around us uneasily, but I'm ignoring her.

'Because I already told you. I like you. And I . . .'

'What is going on here?'

We turn in the direction of the softly spoken question. It's our principal, Mr Roy Lobo. All of us pale.

'We are discussing the pitch,' I blurt out.

'What pitch?' Mr Lobo asks us, his voice cold as steel. The look in his eyes is not reassuring.

Mr Lobo never interacts with any student. Everyone steers clear of him. Keerthi once told me that it was highly likely that he was a vampire because he didn't step out at all during the day.

'Come to my office,' he says and walks away.

The three of us look at one another in horror.

'Should we make a run for it?' Keerthi whispers. 'It's not like he knows our names or which class we're in.'

Mr Lobo turns around and pins us with a smile that turns our blood cold.

'Shut up and follow him,' I mutter.

I can sense Arsalan moving in closer. Even in the middle of this fiasco, I feel my body turn gooey because of his presence.

We follow Mr Lobo. In the antechamber outside his office, his surprised assistant looks at us, not sure what's happening. Mr Lobo settles down behind his desk, and we sit on the chairs before it.

There's a lot of wood panelling everywhere and potted plants that break the monotony. Two windows are flung wide open, bringing in lots of light. Okay, so not a vampire.

Mr Lobo asks us to introduce ourselves. We do so hesitantly. The escape into anonymity option is closed.

'So tell me about this pitch,' he says.

I start to explain the pitch contest.

'Of course, I know about that,' Mr Lobo says, steepling his hands together. 'What's *your* pitch?'

'It's not ready yet,' I tell him.

'Well?' he prompts. 'Show me what you've got.'

I look at Arsalan, surprised at his silence. He is easily the most talkative of us all. Arsalan shrugs and nods slightly as if to tell me to go ahead.

So, taking a deep breath, I begin talking. I explain the idea behind it, the concept of the app and that we have a mock-up of the app ready.

Mr Lobo listens to us in silence. His expression does not change one bit. I am getting a very bad feeling about this. Of course, our pitch isn't really ready. But is what I have said so hopeless?

'Why?' His quiet question cuts through my rambling thoughts.

'I'm sorry?'

'Why do you want to make this?' he asks. 'Henna does not come under essential services. Why would anyone want this?'

I look down at my lap. This is a question I know I need to be prepared to answer. I'm not ashamed. I'm just a little conscious. But I take a deep breath and lift my head.

'My mother started applying henna to brides when I was a small girl,' I begin. 'At first, it was people in the family, but she was so good at it that everyone said she ought to be paid for it.'

I look down again and give a sad chuckle. 'My mother was horrified at that thought. She hated the idea that she was selling a "service".'

I try to decipher Mr Lobo's expression, but I get no dice. I don't look at either Arsalan or Keerthi right now.

'She thought that if she got paid, it would make her financially independent and that meant Abbu wasn't really needed. And my mother would rather die than make my father feel redundant. So, for a long time, she refused the money. But about five years ago, when she saw the time and effort it took, and also because she really needed the income, she started charging money. Small amounts that she would split with my aunts, and they would use it as pocket money. Remember, this was never meant to be serious money. This was just a little extra.'

My face heats when I remember how Ammi would instruct Amal and me to not tell Abbu when she treated us to Magnum ice creams sometimes.

'Recently, something happened that made me change my mind about staying in the background.'

'What?' Mr Lobo asks, sitting forward.

'Ammi had gone to apply henna for a bride, and the bride's mother refused to pay her the full amount. She sent them away after paying just half the amount. That made me really, really mad.'

'So you decided to make the app?' Mr Lobo asks.

I shake my head. 'Actually, I went to the bride's home and confronted the mother. I fought with her and made her pay the rest of the money. Ammi wasn't happy that I'd done it, but it got me thinking that there has to be a way that people would treat her more professionally. Because it may not be a daily essential service, but in India, can you imagine a wedding happening without henna? If wedding planning services are a thing, if beauty and make-up services are important, then why not henna?'

There's silence as I finish. I fidget a little uncomfortably.

Mr Lobo draws in a breath. I brace myself for the worst. He's going to laugh us out of here.

'Abir, I'm very impressed,' he says.

I blink. 'What?'

He nods. 'So, I'm pushing your team,' he looks at the three of us, 'to directly pitch before the jury.'

I can't understand what he means. 'But sir . . .'

'I was anyway going to look through all the proposals. And I'll be observing the selection of the teams that pitch before the jury. Think of it as clearing the first round,' he says, smiling at us. 'But make sure you tell all this when you're pitching before the jury. Everyone loves a good back story. Go now. And don't create so much ruckus in the corridors and grounds.'

Stunned, the three of us leave his office with muttered thanks.

When we're outside, Keerthi and I erupt into squeals. The principal's assistant glares at us, so we stop ourselves.

'Oh my god, oh my god, oh my god!' I squeak as we leave the building. 'I can't believe this!'

I turn to Arsalan, forgetting all our personal mess for the moment. But he doesn't look as happy as I thought he'd be. In fact, he looks pale.

'Are you all right?' I ask him, quickly glancing at Keerthi, who shrugs. We're both so excited, so it makes no sense that he doesn't feel the same.

'Actually,' he clears his throat. 'I . . .'

'Arsalan!'

A high voice calls out from behind us. A car has swept into the drive and a woman gets out of it. She's dressed stylishly in a peach silk saree, her pallu draped 'fashionably', as Ammi might say, instead of wrapped around her shoulders like the women in my family do, making them look like mummies. The Egyptian kind.

There's something familiar about her.

'I thought I'd have to call you, but look! Here you are!' the woman says. 'I was nearby to meet someone for lunch. I thought I'd see if you wanted to join me. I know how much you love Mamagoto.'

The woman is nearer now. My heart speeds up as the penny drops.

'So, are you free, beta?' she asks. She gives Keerthi and me the kind of vapid smile one would give salespeople in a store.

'Shall we go? You're free, right?' she asks.

Arsalan looks miserable. 'I have classes. I'm not free, Ammi,' he says.

Ammi.

Champagne Saree is his mother.

44

'Who's this?' his mother asks, looking at me pointedly. Her eyes narrow, as if she's trying to remember if she's seen me somewhere.

I want to just disappear, but then why should I? Though embarrassment coils into me as I think back to how I'd behaved with her.

'These are my friends,' Arsalan says. 'I'm working on a project with them.'

'Oh, wonderful,' his mother says. She gives me and Keerthi an appraising look.

I suppose for rich people like her, all people who are not similarly fancily dressed are not worth remembering. She probably can't recall that I'm the girl who made her pay up.

Dragging a curious Keerthi, I wave goodbye at Arsalan and his mother. We walk determinedly in the direction of the classrooms. Lunch hour is almost over.

I can feel their gaze on my back. My head is spinning. I have been having these silly fantasies about Arsalan, but now . . .

It makes things easier. Doesn't it? There's no way he and I can ever be together. I have been such an idiot.

'Hold on, Abir. What the hell is going on?' Keerthi asks me, spinning me in the direction of an empty classroom.

A bark of laughter erupts from my mouth, mirthless and filled with pain and embarrassment. Just a while ago, Arsalan had wanted us to come inside one such room where we could 'hash' out our differences. I wonder how things would have gone if he'd told his mother that he wanted to send a proposal to my house. For me.

'Abir, what is going on?' Keerthi asks again.

I pace the length of the room because somehow I feel I have to move. 'So, the story I said inside the principal's office about barging into a house and asking for the rest of the payment?'

She nods, her eyes shining. 'That was such a badass move. Wait, when was this?'

'The day you and I went to Commercial Street,' I remind her.

'You made me miss all that drama and let me sit in a park?' she asks me accusingly. 'So what's that got to do with everything?'

'Guess whose mother that lady is?'

That's when she makes the connection.'Shit. Oh my god. No.'

I shrug. 'I saw him there that day. I didn't know it was his house, and the bride was his sister.'

'Oh man, this day just keeps getting better and better,' she says, eyes wide.

'Really? That's the track you're going to take?' I ask her, annoyed at her obvious enjoyment of the drama.

'I didn't mean it like that,' she says, a little chastened. 'I just thought you know . . .' She shrugs. 'The whole star-crossed lovers thingie . . .'

'For god's sake, Keerthi!' I snap. 'Stop it already. This is real life. There won't be any enemies-to-lovers in my future.'

Her shoulders slump. 'I know, but I thought that you and Arsalan should talk and sort this shit out. Especially given how much you two like each other.'

I look down. 'If I thought that he was unsuitable for me before, I think now it makes it all the more impossible for anything to ever happen between us.'

'Stop troubling me, Luke. I need to speak to Abir first.'

Both Keerthi and I fall silent. Arsalan is outside, but he doesn't know that we're inside this classroom. Keerthi walks towards the door to tell him that we're here when he speaks again.

'As it is, I don't know if she'll ever speak to me. If I now tell her about the reel . . .'

Keerthi and I look at each other in shock. What is he talking about? We both edge closer to the door.

'You were just going to teach her a lesson, right?' Luke says the volume of his voice going up and down.

'It's not like you planned to catch her or shot the video. You just encouraged Rohit to post it.'

My breath catches in my throat.

'Stop talking about that,' Arsalan says. 'She's not in class. Where can she be?'

'Listen, today she saw aunty. She knows who your mother is. I really think that you need to come clean to her.'

There's more?

I want to step outside and confront him, but Keerthi puts a hand on my elbow to stop me.

'Maybe I will. One day. But now I need to talk to her and convince her that I'm nothing like my mother.'

I push past Keerthi and step outside. I bump into Arsalan.

'Abir, I . . .'

'I heard everything,' I tell him.

His face pales. 'Let me explain.'

My mouth flattens in a line. 'Please. Spare me the lies . . .'

Keerthi follows me outside. 'Let's go,' she says, her voice hoarse.

'I can't go to class,' I tell her, unable to meet her gaze. There's a riot of emotions coursing around inside my head.

'Let's go home then,' she says as we walk away.

'You come to my place,' I tell her.

She looks at me in surprise, but her eyes soften. 'Sure. Let's go,' she says.

My heart feels like someone has trodden all over it. But somehow, I have clarity.

I have three things I have to do now: pitch the app and win the funding. Ace my exams and get into the best damn college. And stop the nonsense marriage plans.

Arsalan no longer exists.

45

'If you mention the word drama one more time . . .' I warn Keerthi, who puts her hand up in surrender.

'Sorry, sorry. But you have to admit, all this is just so melodramatic and filmy,' she says, picking at a stray thread on my bedsheet. She has not said even once that my house is quaint although I know she's been thinking it.

'It's not. It's my stupid, messed-up life,' I tell her, trying hard not to sniffle. Keerthi coming home has been strange and weird and nice in a way I hadn't thought possible.

There's a knock on the door. 'Ammi, it's okay. You can come inside,' I call out.

Ammi walks inside, holding a tray.

'Oh yay, more food!' Keerthi says, her eyes wide.

We had come home ravenous. If Ammi had been surprised I'd brought a friend home, she hadn't shown it. She just asked us to sit down for lunch. Keerthi kept moaning about how she'd never eaten the combination of plain white rice, dal, chicken phaal, with pickle and papad because it was hands-down the best combination in the world.

'Aunty, you're a national treasure. There's magic in your hands,' Keerthi declared. Ammi blushed happily at the compliment.

Ammi brings in spicy green peas sundal, which Keerthi has never eaten. This is a recipe Ammi invented when she saw how much Amal and I loved chaat. I'd have this any day over the chaat in any of the Commercial Street shops.

'What is in this?' Keerthi asks as she eats a spoonful. 'There's crunch, there's spice, and there's some mango tanginess also.'

Ammi ruffles Keerthi's hair fondly, like she's five years old. 'You girls enjoy this. I'll bring tea in a bit.'

'Tea! After this!' Keerthi wails. 'Aunty, I'll either go into a food coma or have a food baby.' She pats her stomach, and Ammi looks at her in shock. Ammi doesn't know what any of that means, and she's probably just fixated on the words 'coma' and 'baby'.

'Ammi, we'll come out and have tea in a bit,' I tell her.

Ammi leaves with a faintly worried expression on her face.

'So what are we going to do?' Keerthi asks after she's licked the plate clean.

'About what?'

'About Arsalan.'

'I don't want to talk about him. Ever again.'

She cocks her head. 'I feel like maybe we should give him a chance to explain everything.'

My jaw works. I understand now. Arsalan had always known I was the girl who had barged into his house. And he wanted to humiliate me somehow, and he'd found the perfect way to do it by inveigling himself into my life, making me fall for him.

I have never had a problem acknowledging hard facts, so I face this one squarely. *I have fallen for him.*

I shake my head. 'No. Let's not go there.'

'But Abir,' Keerthi protests, looking at me unhappily. 'Listen, the thing is . . .'

'There's *nothing* happening here, Keerthi. Please, let's forget all this ever happened.'

'Fine. We won't talk about this. But you know what we are going to do?'

'What?' I mumble. 'Please don't tell me to talk to my parents about Sahil. Not today. I can't deal with that.'

She nods. 'Not that. But you're going to tell them about the app and what happened in college today. That the principal loved your idea.'

'Our idea.'

She shakes her head. 'No, Abir. This one's all you. And you're going to ace it. Just do whatever you did today to impress Lobo.'

Think about the positives, I tell myself. *Think about all the stuff that is going right. Everything else will fall into place on its own.*

Keerthi's phone rings, and she frowns. 'My mother.'

She answers the phone. 'Yes, yes, Ma. I texted you, right? I told you I'm going to Abir's.'

She's silent for a bit. 'Well, tell him we're sorry. Abir won't be coming to my place any time soon.'

Arsalan had gone to *her* house? He must have assumed we'd go there when we left college.

'Yeah, tell him to go home. I don't want to see him either,' she says and hangs up.

She looks at me. I look at her.

My phone pings. I feel a little gratified. So, he's texted me, and now I can ignore him.

Keerthi picks up my phone and reads the text and shows me the screen.

I can explain everything. Please can we talk?

I take the phone from her and block his number.

46

'Look, my therapist says that sometimes the best way to find peace . . .'

'Hold on. You have a therapist?' I ask Keerthi, surprised.

She nods. 'Since I was thirteen,' she explains. 'Anyway, as I was saying, this thing between you and Ars—'

'Stop right there,' I tell her. We're sitting at the edge of the outdoor basketball court because there's a match happening between our college and another.

She sighs. And then nods in a direction I refuse to look at. I know Arsalan is sitting there as well.

The past month has been torturous. He turns up everywhere I go, trying to talk to me and explain what happened, but I've moved on. The one time I spoke to him, I told him that, but he has clearly decided he is going to keep trying.

'But you have to give him points for trying so hard,' she insists.

I don't answer. It's a warm day in mid-February. The trees in the college campus have burst into bright blooms. The sight sets my heart soaring, but there is still something inside my chest, like a vise. Everything is transient, like the pretty flowers in spring. Today, we're here. And once we finish our exams, we'll all be on our way somewhere else.

The pitch is ready. I've worked on the powerpoint presentation obsessively. It's my dream. I'm going to make it happen.

My parents had been surprised and pleased when I told them what the principal had said. Their willingness to believe authority figures meant that they suddenly started giving more importance to the pitch. Marriage has not been mentioned since I said I wanted to discuss it after the pitch and my exams. I haven't called off the thing with Sahil yet because I know things will go batshit crazy at home once I do.

Let me finish my exams and this pitch, I tell myself.

'Abir,' Keerthi persists like an annoying bee in my ear.

'What?' I sigh.

'Just listen to him once at least. The poor fellow hasn't seen even one moment of the match. He's been staring at you all along.'

'That's not my problem,' I tell her.

'At least, let him help with the pitch. It's . . .'

'You're there, no?' I snap. 'Why do we need him? What's his contribution been for all this, apart from being our designated driver?' I know this is unfair, because he did a lot of the coding too.

Keerthi's face flushes with embarrassment as she looks over my shoulder. I stiffen. I know it's him.

I don't want to look at him, but I turn around.

My first thought is that he looks devastatingly handsome, as always, and I squash it firmly. The second is that he's heard me call him a driver, but he doesn't look mad. He still looks determined.

'Please, Abir. Can we talk?'

I can't carry on walking around college, wondering if he's going to jump out of some corner and try to talk to me. I need to get this over with so I can go back to being mad at him. So, I nod.

I get up. 'Let's go somewhere private,' I tell him, belatedly realizing how suggestive that sounds. To his credit, he ignores it.

We walk quietly to the spot where he and Luke had taken us the day they told us their pitch. We sit on the bench with a good distance between us. The silence is unsettling.

'How's the pitch coming along?' he asks.

I consider him coldly. 'You'll get credit. Don't worry.'

'As a designated driver? Sure, cool,' he deadpans, almost looking like the Arsalan of old.

I roll my eyes. 'It's going fine. But Arsalan, I don't want you to keep stalking me. That's why I said we can talk and get this over with.'

His expression changes slightly. 'I just want to explain, Abir.'

I fold my arms and look at him.

'That day, when you came to my house, I saw you. You walked out of my house, looking so furious and self-righteous.'

I knew it! He'd seen me.

'I spoke to my mother and asked her what happened. She told me how some young girl had come to extort money from her. That just made me so angry,' he says. 'I believed my mother.'

My mouth drops open. Wow, his mother is a piece of work.

'And that you must have been the girl who did all that.'

'Why? Why did you just assume that?' I snap.

'Have you met you?' he asks, a wry smile on his face. He puts his hands up in a conciliatory gesture.

'I was furious, and I decided to try and do something to make you pay for it. I hadn't decided what, but then . . .'

'But then I fell into your arms and your buddies made it into a reel and put it on Instagram,' I finish the sentence.

He folds his arms and looks down. 'I thought it was perfect. But I was wrong. I saw the look on your face when you saw the reel in the canteen and I realized . . .'

'That you didn't want to be associated with someone like me. I get it,' I finish the sentence huffily.

'I really, really thought you were smarter than that,' he says slowly.

I turn to him angrily. 'You're saying I'm dumb?'

He shrugs. 'If the shoe fits. I got the video taken off because I didn't want to make you that sort of online target, and I knew it could get you into trouble.'

'But you *wanted* to get me into trouble, right?' I ask, turning to him. He looks back at me steadily.

'Not any more,' he says.

'Why?'

'A couple of days after the wedding, my sister told me what happened. I couldn't believe my mother would do something like that. I've always known she can be a bit dismissive of people who she thinks are not of her social class, but that's also because she's always overcompensating for not coming from a rich family herself. She feels like this is how she needs to behave to be accepted in her circle. I don't like to think the worst of my mother. I want to think of her as someone who wouldn't take advantage of . . . of . . .' He looks confused as he tries to think of what word he could use to describe my mother.

I stiffen a little. *Really? Champagne Saree wasn't born with a diamond-encrusted spoon in her mouth?*

He looks down for a moment and then looks up. 'But there was another reason, too. I realized that I liked you, a lot. I liked everything about you. How fierce you are, how fearless, how committed. My sister told me she apologized to your mother on our behalf, and I knew that she wouldn't have done that if she didn't think you'd been right.'

I don't know how to respond to that, so I look down at my hands.

'Abir, everything after that day has been true, including what I feel for you.'

I know I shouldn't want to believe his words so badly but I do. I do want to believe him. Then I think of Champagne Saree.

'Well, your mother hates me.'

There's silence. I can't make myself look at him. But I sense him moving closer.

When I look up, his face is serious, and there's a dark intensity in his eyes that makes my insides turn into mush.

'Who cares?' he whispers, before he leans closer to kiss me.

47

I nearly push him away, but then his hands slip down to hold my arms. I don't know how, but my arms are wound around his neck, and then we're kissing.

My body feels like it has opened up somehow, giving me a sense of freedom I've never felt before.

My mind doesn't give up just yet. It pulls me back, snapping me into place after just a few moments of this kiss that I never want to end. *This is his making-out spot. I'm just another girl he's brought here to kiss.*

I push him away. I stand up. My hands are shaking.

'I'm not going to be among the other girls you bring here to kiss, Arsalan!' I tell him, my mouth trembling with the heat of his kiss.

He stands up too, narrowing his eyes. 'What other girls?'

'Your harem of willing girls who come here to . . .'

He turns me around to face him and shakes his head. 'That's rubbish. I don't have a *harem* and I don't bring girls here to kiss. I . . .'

But I'm already striding away.

'Abir,' he calls out.

I pause but don't turn back. 'What?'

'Is this about Sahil?' he asks stiffly.

I turn around, unable to keep the incredulous expression from my face. 'Sahil?'

He nods. 'Yes. Your family accepted his proposal, right?'

'I don't want to talk about him,' I tell him stiffly.

Arsalan looks troubled. 'I know your family likes him, but . . .' He swallows nervously. 'Don't throw away what we have.'

'What we have?' I repeat softly as he walks up to me swiftly.

He nods. A part of me wants to reassure him that I have no plans of marrying Sahil. Now or ever. But I don't owe him any answers. I don't owe him anything. Yet, I do feel that I should think this through before I respond with anger.

'I don't know what we have, Arsalan. I need to think this through. Can you give me time to do that?'

When I walk away this time, he doesn't stop me.

How can I trust him? How can I know for sure that he's not lying? By giving him another chance, by letting him show he means what he's saying. But who has the time for that? Our exams are happening soon, and the pitch is even before that. After that, we all go our separate ways. For all I know, he's not going to stick around. He could be planning to study abroad, like everyone else I know.

Keerthi is too. The thought that Keerthi and Arsalan will go abroad and study in prestigious universities while I continue to struggle is not comforting, but I'm not in the mood for a pity party. I want to get away before Keerthi spots me and grills me about what happened.

Luck is with me. I leave college before Keerthi can find me. But my luck runs out when I reach home and find Samreen Khala seated with Ammi, deep in conversation.

Samreen Khala used to be my favourite aunt. Now, every time I see her, I feel a jolt of fear. All thanks to that stupid Sahil and his refusal to halt the juggernaut he's set in motion.

'Come, come and sit here,' Samreen Khala beckons me warmly. Clearly, if Sahil had told her to call this off, her expression would have been very different. It's all on me again.

I can still feel the pressure of Arsalan's lips on mine as I sit down.

'What's going on with you? I hardly see you around these days,' she says.

'Abir is busy with the exams and that . . . what's it called?' Ammi frowns.

'The pitch,' I tell her dully.

Ammi nods and explains what I've been doing to Samreen Khala. She's especially proud that the principal liked my idea so much. Even Samreen Khala is mighty impressed.

'Wow, that's great, Abir,' she says. An eyebrow goes up, because she knows how much Sahil helped me in this. She thinks she's facilitating a great love story. She draws in a great breath. 'I'm here to talk about your engagement.'

My blood turns to ice. It's now or never.

'I don't want to marry him,' I blurt out.

The silence between us stretches and thins.

'No one is getting you married *now*,' Samreen Khala assures me. Ammi looks a little embarrassed, as if I spoke out of turn at an important event.

I draw in a breath. 'I don't want to marry him *ever*.'

Ammi and Samreen Khala look at each other. I can see thoughts transmitting between them. I'm bonkers or stressed or whatever because I can't surely be serious.

'Why?' Samreen Khala asks me finally. There's the slightest hint of aggression in her voice that *I* am rejecting her brother-in-law.

'I don't *want* to marry him.'

Ammi gasps and looks like she wants to shake some sense into me.

I turn to her quickly and shake my head. 'I don't want this. I don't want to be betrothed to him for however many years in the future you all are planning my marriage. I don't want to marry him ever.'

Samreen Khala's nostrils flare. 'Why? What's wrong with him?'

'Nothing is wrong with him. I am not interested in thinking about marriage right now. I have too much going on.'

'Apa, this is not done,' Samreen Khala addresses Ammi. 'What will I tell my family? I will lose face. Especially after Sahil expressed his desire to marry her, and . . .'

Ammi's forehead has broken out in a sweat.

'I didn't say anything all these days because I was busy and because all of you were not discussing it. But if you're going to start talking about engagements, I can't. I just can't. Other girls my age are figuring out their university plans and careers. I will not be someone who is planning my trousseau instead.'

I get up and walk away. Near my room door, I turn around. 'I am not going to change my mind. And I'm sorry if this puts you in a tough spot, Khala, but you should have asked me if I wanted to marry him instead of assuming that I would.'

I step into my room and shut the door, aware that I've just lobbed a bomb. Now I have to watch everything explode.

48

The atmosphere at home is funereal. Nani is confused, but she has not asked me what's wrong. Abbu and Ammi are both giving me the silent treatment.

But I'll survive it.

At dinner, I make up my plate and try to move to my room without making eye contact with anyone.

Abbu's voice cuts across the room like a whip. 'Abir!'

I turn slowly. If I'd thought it would just be the silent treatment, I'd been wrong, obviously.

'Come here.'

I walk back to the dining table, my heart thudding as I take in his grim expression. I think back to the time when I was smaller and he'd pick me up from the middle of the floor after he came home from the shop and whirl me around while I squealed in delight.

Ammi is studiously staring at her plate. She refuses to meet my eyes, her face closed off in anxiety and disappointment. Nani looks at us impassively, but I can sense the compassion in her eyes. Amal is watching the proceedings wide-eyed.

Abbu clears his throat. 'I want you to know that your decisions affect other people too. You will be ruining not just your life but your sister's as well,' he announces.

When you are sisters, apparently, your fates are somehow tied together. I'm aware that it's a guilt trap, and I refuse to fall for it.

'Amal will be fine,' I respond softly, glad my voice is not shaking.

'And you have no worries about how this will look to the world? To other families? To people in our community?'

These words fuel my rising anger and let me say what I'd thought would be impossible.

'Why should it? I'm living my life. Why should what I do affect other people? I'm just asking to be left alone so I can study like everyone else.'

Abbu's face is grim. 'You know what they say about educating girls too much? And giving all these girls so much freedom that they are riding around the city on their scooties at all hours of the night?'

I've never been afraid of my father, but I've always held back, unwilling to fight with him or create any sort of rift at home. I've chosen the easy way out. But now the time for sitting on the fence is long gone.

Abbu continues, for these are rhetorical questions to which he expects no answer. 'Educating girls too much creates all sorts of headaches. Finding the right match for them becomes all the more difficult.'

The misogyny in that sentence blows me away. I speak up, aware that my voice is not as strong as I'd like it to be. 'I want to study and make something of my life. I don't want to be tied down by getting married and having in-laws.'

Abbu looks livid. 'We are not getting you married right *now*. So what's the harm in giving your consent to this? It will be years till you get married.'

'What if we change our minds in those years? I don't want to tie down Sahil, especially because I don't think I will ever love him or want to marry him.'

Abbu's face blanches because I've said that awful word, 'love'.

Ammi finally meets my gaze. She licks her lips nervously. 'Abir, you will fall in love with Sahil after you marry him.'

Abbu shoots her an incredulous look. To my surprise, she doesn't back down. 'And isn't all of this romantic, the way he asked for your hand and all that?'

'I didn't ask for any of this! If he truly cared for me, he would have asked me if I wanted this. He would have respected my wishes,' I tell her. 'I don't want to have a fiancé. I don't want to go through years of my life engaged to someone.'

Abbu looks weary. 'Let her go, Shahana. She will regret this later. And she's being selfish and thoughtless. How we will ever face your sister and her in-laws, I don't know. She has embarrassed us and . . .'

There's nothing left for me to say, so I walk away. Abbu is talking about me as if I am not there.

After dinner, Amal comes into our bedroom.

'Api?' she says when I look up at her and then go back to working out maths problems. If my family's machinations don't kill me, then differentiation will.

'What?'

'Keerthi texted me, asking why your phone is switched off.'

I look up at her, exasperated. I switched off my phone the moment I left college. I haven't switched it on, though I have been very tempted to see if Arsalan reached out to me.

I pick up my phone, but Amal stops me. 'Wait. I want to talk to you before that,' she says and shuts the door.

'I'm not in the mood, Amal,' I tell her curtly.

She ignores me and sits down at the edge of the bed gingerly.

'Won't you reconsider this . . . this thing with Sahil? Ammi was saying that Samreen Khala hasn't yet broken the news to her in-laws. Maybe she's hoping we can . . .'

I shake my head vehemently. 'I don't want this. I'm sure of it.'

'But why?' she asks.

I look at my sister. I can't tell her that fifty percent of my problem is because I have feelings for someone else.

'I want to be free to live my life the way I want. Is that too much to ask?'

'Fine,' she nods. 'I'm scared of Abbu, but I'm with you. Whatever you decide.'

She leaves the room. With a sigh, I switch on my phone, aware that Keerthi is waiting for details about my talk with Arsalan.

'Abir Maqsood. How *dare* you switch off your phone after disappearing off with Arsalan into the bushes?'

Too late, I realize that her call had connected as soon as I switched on the phone and that she was on speaker.

Too late for me since Ammi had walked into the room.

49

Ammi shuts the door behind her and walks up to me even as Keerthi goes on and on about Arsalan. I quickly hit the end button, and her voice ends on a squawk.

She looks furious. 'What was she talking about?'

I try not to quail under her glare, but I'm unable to keep my gaze level with hers. She sits down on the bed, her hands over her mouth.

'*This* is why you don't want to marry Sahil!' she says in a hushed, broken voice, her eyes filling with tears.

I shake my head furiously. 'No, Ammi. My reasons for not marrying Sahil are the same. I don't want to think about marriage and everything just yet. I want to focus on my education and my future.'

'Then who is this boy? This *Arsalan?*' Ammi asks, her voice cracking.

I don't know how to make my mother understand these overflowing feelings I have for Arsalan and how they're juxtaposed with my desire to do something with my life. And how there's no space for Sahil in any of this whatsoever.

'Remember that scene in *DDLJ*? That mother-daughter scene?' I ask her suddenly.

'The one where her father overhears everything and takes her back to India to get married to the boy of his choice?' My mother asks sarcastically.

It is that scene.

'What about it?' Ammi asks.

'I just didn't think I'd feel . . .'

I don't know how to continue this conversation without dying of embarrassment. On cue, Keerthi's number flashes on my phone again. Before I can cut the call, Ammi picks it up and answers it on speaker.

'Keerthi, who is Arsalan?' she asks.

There's silence on the other end when Keerthi realizes what has happened.

'Aunty, he's our classmate,' she says finally.

Ammi glowers at me. 'I knew I should have put her in an all-girls college. Why did I even enroll her here?' she mutters. 'What's going to happen?'

'Aunty, nothing will happen,' Keerthi assures her.

'Also, it's not like Abir and Arsalan are getting married any time soon. They're just kids. And he's after all the son of that client who tricked you out of your money . . .'

Ammi covers her mouth again in shock. 'What?' she gasps. I lick my dry lips and nod.

'Keerthi, I'll talk to you later,' I tell her and hit the end button.

Ammi and I stare at each other. I don't know what is going on in her head any more than she can read my mind. I really hope to god she can't read my mind. Then she'll know that I kissed Arsalan. Not once, but twice.

'Do you even know what you've done?' she asks finally.

'I didn't do anything,' I tell her, lying blatantly. 'I mean, I didn't . . . he . . . he said he likes me and . . .'

I'm blushing like a tomato. Where's badass Abir when she needs to be here?

Ammi covers her cheeks with her palms. 'Bas. Don't tell me anything more.'

'Ammi, please. Just listen to me,' I plead with her.

'What do I listen to, Abir? I never thought you'd do something like this,' she whispers.

'I didn't do anything,' I say with conviction.

'If word gets out, our family will be disgraced, even more once they know that you rejected Sahil for this boy.'

'I didn't do that. I am not getting married to anyone right now.'

But Ammi doesn't seem to hear a word of what I've said. 'Just imagine. They'll make fun of us when they hear it. A mehendiwali's daughter getting married into that high and mighty family. We'll be the butt of all jokes.'

I grit my teeth. 'Ammi, just for a moment, can you put yourself in my shoes?'

She pauses her rambling and looks at me. 'What do you mean?'

'I'm good at what I do, Ammi. I'm going to ace that pitch. I'm going to top the class in the exams. I have all these big dreams of what I want to do. Please don't tell me you think that in this day and age, it's pointless for me to have these dreams because I am a girl.'

Ammi is silent as she considers my words.

'As for Arsalan, I already told him nothing can happen between us. He . . .' I blush as I continue, but I have to say them anyway. 'He's not like his mother. And he really likes me. But I don't plan to get married to him either. We're just . . . we're just kids. So, Ammi, will you be on my side? You understand why I'm doing this, right?'

I'd hoped to see a transformation on Ammi's face but there's nothing. Disappointment fills me, but then she speaks up.

'I just want what's best for you.'

I nod. 'I know that. I'm trying so hard to study and succeed and fulfil my dreams.'

Her expression falters. 'Your dreams were my dreams too, Abir.'

I frown. 'What do you mean?'

She gazes into the distance. I think she's transported back to the past when she'd been my age. She had gotten married just after she finished her PUC exams.

239

'I wanted to get a fine arts degree,' she says softly.

I gasp. I used to think that Ammi was naturally artistic, not that it was something she had actively wanted to pursue.

'Then?'

'Abba was very reluctant. Back then, there was only Chitrakala Parishath, and I knew he would never agree because it was a co-ed college.'

'So you just got married to Abbu?' I ask.

'I snuck away from home one day and got the admission form, filled it out and submitted it,' she says.

What?

She gives me a tiny smile.

'And then?'

'I got in, of course.'

'Of course. And then you gave up and got married to Abbu.'

She casts me a withering look. 'His proposal had come, and Abba agreed, and the marriage was fixed. I …' She licks her lips nervously.

'What?' I'm breathless with anticipation.

'I got his number and called him, and I told him I wanted to study, even after marriage.'

I clap my hand over my mouth. I may have kissed Arsalan and broken an engagement, but hello, we're Gen Z. We bring chaos wherever we go. But for Ammi to do this!

'And Abbu said no?' I ask when she doesn't continue.

She smiles and shakes her head. 'He said, sure.'

'What?'

She nods. 'Yeah, but we decided to keep it a secret between us. We got married, and I attended classes for some months.'

Was this the rebellion that Nani had referred to? In Ammi's days, this would have been quite ground-breaking. I wait, not wanting to prompt her with the wrong words again. But she doesn't say anything.

'Ammi? Then?'

'I dropped out when I got pregnant,' she says.

I pale. 'You mean you didn't complete your education because of me?'

She rolls her eyes. 'I was already considering it, Abir. It wasn't easy managing a home, attending classes in secret and being answerable to everyone at home. We hadn't told anyone except Ammi that I was studying. It was chaotic. I was relieved at one level when I found out I was pregnant.'

I process her words in silence for a few moments. 'So why were you pushing me to get married to Sahil when you very well know this can happen?'

Her face flushes a deep red. 'Because I thought he would be supportive, like your Abbu. I don't want you getting married into a family where you have to navigate through family politics and not get to do what you want.'

'So a supportive husband will be helpful, you're saying?'

She nods, her eyes lighting up hopefully, but they dim when she sees me shake my head firmly.

'I don't need Sahil or anyone's support, apart from yours and Abbu's, to fulfill my dreams, Ammi. I'm enough on my own.'

She breathes out heavily and gets up.

'Your exams are next month. We'll talk about all this once that's done,' she says and walks away.

I look at her departing figure and shut my eyes. Listening to what she'd been through helped me see things a little better, but it has just made my resolve firmer. And I don't know if she's going to support me, but then I hadn't planned on telling her anything about Arsalan.

Stupid Keerthi.

I dial her number, and she answers warily.

'Shit. I'm sorry. So sorry!' she mumbles. 'What happened? What did aunty say?'

'Don't even ask,' I mutter.

'Oh god, Abir. What's going to happen now?' she asks.

'I wish I knew,' I tell her honestly.

Is Ammi going to rat me out to Abbu in a bid to bring me back under control? She's only told me to study for my exams. But what happens once the exams are over?

End game.

50

On the day of the pitch, I wake up with a screaming throat.

No, no, no, I panic. This can't be happening. I hop out of bed, gargle repeatedly with hot salt water, and the pain recedes.

I had a slight cold just two days ago, but I hadn't paid attention to it. My ears and throat had been hurting a little last night, but I was so busy going over the slides of the presentation that I ignored it.

In the two weeks since I had refused to get engaged to Sahil, things have been eerily calm. Samreen Khala stopped coming over to our house. Abbu barely speaks to me, and I do the same. We're at an impasse.

The study holidays started two days after that basketball match, so I have not been to college. In those two days, I'd avoided Arsalan as best as I could.

I have to say, I am quite pleased that he has respected my request to give me time to think things through. I am so used to my family not paying my wishes any attention.

Today, Keerthi and I pitch before the jury. Our pitch is the only one that has been selected from the junior college. This fills me with equal amounts of dread and exhilaration. Quite a few people from our class will be coming today to be a part of the audience. Students from other colleges are also coming to observe.

I haven't given much thought to what it will mean to look out at the huge audience. I have just focussed on the presentation and what I need to say.

'What is going on?' Amal yawns as she wakes up and finds me gargling.

Ammi and Nani, who are reading the Quran at the dining table, glance at me in concern.

'I think you should go back to bed,' Ammi says.

'Ammi! I can't,' I croak. This is the first time I have spoken since morning, and I am shocked at how my voice sounds.

'Clearly, you'll not be able to present,' she says.

'I'll manage,' I whisper, because that's the only volume at which I can speak now.

Amal leaves for school as I collect everything I need. My heart is thudding. I set the steamer and sit before it, hoping it will work its magic and some of my voice will return.

Nani shuffles forward and places a fistful of lozenges on the table. 'This might help,' she says.

Still sitting, I hug her waist, her soft stomach, such a comfort. It's odd how I don't feel this comfortable hugging my parents, but with Nani, it's something else.

'Go, do your best,' she says, ruffling my hair. Nani has been quietly supportive since the big fight. She had come to my room and told me that she doesn't understand why I have to do this, but if I want it badly enough, she's with me.

Ammi places a thermos on the table. I look at her in surprise. 'Hot lemon and ginger water to soothe your throat,' she explains.

I nod and get up. I want to hug her too, but she's still stilted around me.

I get ready. *Why did this have to happen today? Why couldn't my throat have locked up tomorrow? Or even tonight?*

I look at myself in the mirror. I look terrible. Still, I try to salvage whatever I can when all I want to do is curl up under my comforter and go back to sleep.

I wave goodbye to Ammi and Nani, not wanting to test my voice.

When I walk out of the house, Abbu is standing next to his scooter.

'Come, I'll drop you,' he says gruffly.

Did my family have to choose today to be nice to me? I feel like bursting into tears, so I just nod and pretend like it's not a big deal.

I settle myself behind him but don't hold on to his shoulder like I would normally do. He fixes his helmet and hands me the spare.

When we stop at a signal, he says gruffly, 'Do your best today, beta.'

I sniffle and nod.

'You think I don't know how hard your mother works. I've been seeing it for years. It makes me feel bad that I haven't given her the comfortable life that she deserves. And then I see you, making this app to help her, and I am both proud and ashamed. Proud of you that you are not self-centred and that you want to make things better for your mother. And ashamed that I couldn't do better for you either.'

I'm stunned. I don't say anything because the signal changes and Abbu moves forward. But I am filled with joy that this app that I've been hoping to develop means so much for everyone involved.

As college approaches, I put my hand on his shoulder and squeeze. He turns his head slightly and smiles. I smile back.

My throat may still be on fire, but my heart is tonnes lighter.

51

'**Y**ou're going to have to do this,' I mouth at Keerthi. There is hardly any sound coming out. Despite sucking on at least five lozenges, my throat seems to have worsened since I came to college.

She shakes her head. 'No! Abir, I can't! This is your baby!'

We're sitting in an empty classroom. The last time we were here, we overheard Arsalan and Luke talking about me.

Arsalan was the first person I saw as soon as I walked through the college gates. Our eyes met, and I looked away. My heart ached for some reason. But I had more important things to focus on.

Keerthi is looking more and more frantic. 'I thought I'd have to just be your support person. Look at the way I'm dressed!' she yelps. She's looking fine, neater than she normally does.

I can't speak because it hurts too much now. I shrug. 'I can't make the pitch like this,' I mouth. No sound comes out, but a new shard of pain slices through my vocal cords.

'Shit. Shit. Shit,' she moans and holds her head in her hands.

This is not going to work. She is falling apart.

I take a deep breath and prod her so that she looks at me. 'Call Arsalan,' I mouth.

She looks at me sharply. 'Are you sure?' she asks.

I nod. There's no other option. He's technically still part of the team.

I sit back on the chair and shut my eyes as she leaves. My throat hurts so much.

I sense his presence before I even open my eyes.

'We've got this,' he says. 'We won't let you down.'

I nod. He and Keerthi go through the slides and discuss the best ways to present the pitch.

Since I have nothing else to do, I sit and drink in his features. Strangely, it makes me feel better.

Keerthi is still nervous and twitchy, but Arsalan seems calm.

As we leave the classroom, Arsalan says, 'A word, Abir.'

'I'll set this up,' Keerthi says and skips off with the laptop and notes.

Arsalan takes my hand. My fingers tremble, and then I return the pressure.

'Abir, the way I feel about you, it's not going to change or go away.' A ghost of a smile touches his lips. 'This is also probably the safest time to tell you since you can't yell at me.'

I pull away my hand and stare at him. Everything that has happened all my life — my fight for the freedom to make my own choices, all the arguments at home — have led to this moment.

'I am probably infectious, and you will also fall sick,' I croak. And then I go on tiptoes and kiss his cheek.

The look on his face is incredulous.

The bell rings most unhelpfully, and we race to the auditorium. We find the seats that Keerthi has saved for us in the front row with the other participants.

I sit in a daze — illness, misery, stress about the pitch and happiness make a strange cocktail — through the introductions. The jury members are a decent bunch of names from the IT industry, from start-ups that went on to get big funding. The principal is sitting nearby, arms folded. As if he can sense my gaze, he turns his head and nods at me once.

When the pitches begin, my nervousness ratchets up. I try not to focus on the other pitches. Some of them are so bad, I don't know how they managed to reach this stage! The jury members aren't impressed and a couple of them are downright rude as they shred the proposals.

Arsalan leans close and whispers in my ear, 'I imagine Luke and I would have been among this lot.' he says.

My fingers move over my phone screen.

I grin, and he looks startled. 'I made you laugh!' he says.

> You chose a fine day to be chatty.
> When I can't reply.

He reads the message and grins in response.

And then it's our turn.

Our classmates let out a cheer of excitement and encouragement. I get up on the stage with Arsalan and Keerthi and take over the set up by connecting the laptop to the projector. The other participants had loaded their presentations on a pen drive that was plugged into the auditorium computer. But we wanted to run the prototype app, and it was easier to do this on Keerthi's laptop where all the dummy data was loaded.

Butterflies as large as predatory birds flap around in my belly as I look over at the expectant faces of the audience. This is it.

I hit enter.

Arsalan starts speaking. He will set the scene for the pitch and explain why we made this app. But instead, his words are about me.

'The creator of this app is Abir Maqsood. Her mother started applying henna to brides from the time Abir was small. And five years ago, she started doing this professionally.'

I stare at Arsalan. I had included my mother's story in the pitch, but much later in the sequence because I was self-conscious and I didn't want to make the whole thing about *me*.

'A few months ago, Abir's mother came to my home to apply henna for my sister who was getting married. Instead of paying her dues, my mother sent her away after paying her just half. It was this that inspired Abir's desire to build an app to ensure that individual entrepreneurs, artisans and people in the service industry could be protected from harassment and abuse.'

I am in shock.

Keerthi moves me to the side and takes over the laptop duties as she starts showing the audience how the app is supposed to work, which plays out on the screen even as Arsalan continues to talk.

There's a hushed silence in the auditorium. The jury members are sitting straight, and one is leaning forward. Mr Lobo looks at us through narrowed eyes.

Arsalan succinctly narrates the story of how we built the app and who played what role. He ends by explaining that I have laryngitis.

'This is Abir's app. Her story. And her determination that has brought us here. But she's down today, and the two of us have stepped in to present in her stead. We hope you will see the promise and potential in the app and in Abir,' Arsalan ends.

There's silence and then thunderous applause, of a kind not a single participant has received. I tear up and hug Keerthi. Arsalan looks on with a faint smile. I don't have the words—or voice—to thank him for he had presented it far, far better than I could have dreamt of.

As we walk away, someone tells us that the jury members want to meet us in the principal's office.

We wait nervously in Mr Lobo's office.

'What do you think they'll tell us?' Keerthi whispers from my left.

Arsalan shrugs at my right. 'Who knows, Keerthi?'

I know that whatever happens, we did this. We accomplished something. Whether or not our app is chosen for funding, we did this once, and we can do it again. Hard work has led us here. But luck might just push us over the edge.

I am also very aware of Arsalan, who is close to me. He and I can't stop looking at each other. I don't want to marry *anyone* right now. But I would like to have him in my life and maybe in a few years, after I finish college and post-graduate and have worked for a while . . . who knows?

I find myself smiling, and he smiles back, reaching out to hold my hand.

The door opens, and the jury members walk inside, led by Mr Lobo whose impassive face gives nothing away.

When everyone is seated, I realize my hands are clenched in tight fists.

'Of all the pitches that we heard today, yours is the one that showed the most promise,' the woman who heads the jury begins. 'And we would like to offer you a funding of . . .'

EPILOGUE

Birthdays are celebrated quietly in my family, with small useful presents and a bowl of kheer. It's always an excuse for someone super religious to start talking about how birthdays are actually marking off another year that brings us closer to our death.

So when Abbu, of all people, tells me on the morning of my birthday that there's a surprise waiting for me outside, I'm filled with dread. The concept of surprises is unknown in our family.

'Come, Api!' Amal says.

I slide off the chair reluctantly. I am tired. Ever since we won the pitch, the pressure of work has gone up dramatically. Actually building the app is not easy. Keerthi moved out of the country for her undergraduate studies in August, so it's just been me. And Arsalan.

I walk towards the door. Ammi follows, looking nervous but pleased.

'Do you know what this is about?' I whisper.

She shakes her head. But I can see her smile, and I know that she knows.

When we step outside into the small space that separates our house from the narrow, noisy street, there is a shiny gift-wrapped box on the ground.

'It's because you are now eighteen,' Abbu says.

I pick up the box and put it on a stool that's appeared by my side all of a sudden.

I smile at him uncertainly. I unwrap the box. Something shiny peers at me from inside.

'What's this?' I ask.

'See for yourself,' Nani says, looking very pleased too.

I pull out the shiny round thing. And then frown because it's a pink helmet.

'A helmet?' *Why does everyone think I need a helmet?*

Abbu has disappeared. *Where did he go?*

'It's not just a helmet,' Ammi says with a soft smile on her face.

Things have been settling down in the house since the app was funded, but they are still a little uneasy. It's like we are all coming to terms with all the change that's happening.

Here's the other thing: now that Keerthi is gone, Ammi's the only one who knows about Arsalan and me. And I don't know if that's a good thing or a bad thing.

Our gate creaks open, and I look up.

Abbu is wheeling a shiny new purple scooter through the gate.

My heart races in shock. *Is this what I think this is? No, it can't be.*

I've heard my family talk about other people who *let* their daughters run around the city on scooters and how disdainful my parents are about them.

'You've made us very proud,' Ammi says.

Abbu doesn't say anything, but he pulls out the key from the ignition and hands it to me.

My mouth drops open. 'Ammi, Abbu, what is this?'

'What does it look like?' Amal says with a short screech as she jumps up and down. 'They got you a scooter for your birthday!'

I look at my parents' faces to see if this is real. And it is.

Abbu picks up my hand and drops the keys into my palm and then folds my fingers over.

'It's yours. You deserve it,' he says quietly.

A scooter isn't just a scooter. It means freedom— the kind I didn't think I'd ever get, the kind that I didn't believe my family would be capable of allowing me.

A scooter of my own means no more haggling with autos, no more waiting for buses, and if need be, I can even drop Ammi off at her henna appointments. I can do all the 'running around' that is usually done by men and boys and sons in the family. I can be independent.

Abbu's eyes turn a little dark. 'I know you won't misuse the freedom I'm giving you, Abir,' he says solemnly.

I nod, because I won't.

But I think of Arsalan, who happened to get admission in the same college as me, whose birthday texts to me led to a hushed conversation that lasted for an hour past midnight and who I know is waiting for me in college at this moment. And I know, that maybe I will.

Just a wee bit.

Andaleeb Wajid is a hybrid author, having published more than forty novels in the past fourteen years. Andaleeb enjoys writing in a number of different genres such as young adult, romance and horror. Andaleeb's romance trilogy Jasmine Villa Series was published in February 2023.

Read more by Andaleeb Wajid

'Leaving you and the kids. Khudahafiz.'

That was all the Post-it on the fridge said. Since then, the sole focus of Maria's life has been to find her mother and bring her home so that life could go back to normal. But as Maria grapples with a house in shambles, an angry father, a sullen brother, and her growing attraction for the class hero, the Basketball Guy, she slowly uncovers clues about Ammi's disappearance. Was Ammi truly the loving mother she had believed her to be?

An insightful and funny tale of growing up with a single parent from Andaleeb Wajid.

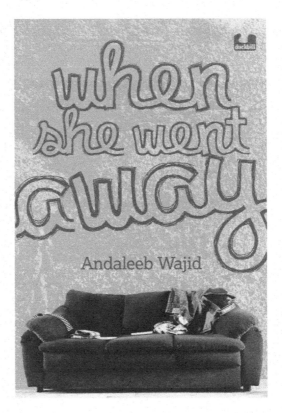

Read the opening of *When She Went Away*

My mother woke up one morning, decided she'd had enough of living her life with us and left. That's right. She just left.

We woke up to see our breakfasts laid out on the dining table and our school lunches packed neatly by the side. Abbu's office lunch was also in a box by his chair. We looked around everywhere, Abbu worried and confused at first, Saud scared, and I, with a feeling like a block of ice in my stomach.

We called her number many times, but it was always switched off.

Abbu called up Ammi's sister to ask if she was there, if there had been any emergency, all the while wondering what emergency would make her leave without telling us. Seema Khala was surprised and shocked. Ammi wasn't there.

Abbu then called Ammi's brother, Feroze Mamu, who told us that Ammi wasn't at his house either.

I don't think I've ever seen Abbu as frantic as he'd been that day.

He paced up and down, muttering to himself, and forgot to send us to school. Not that we were planning to go, anyway. Saud, who was thirteen then, started sniffling and I wanted to hit him hard. I wanted him to shut up so I could think.

Ammi put up all her reminders to Abbu on the fridge. Like 'Pay school fees' or 'Cable rent due'. I'd once wondered if this was how they communicated about everything, and then, of course, I'd quickly started to think about other stuff because I never paid much attention to my parents. Who did?

There was a new note on the fridge that day. I pulled it from under the fat strawberry magnet and read it carefully before handing it to Abbu. In her usual, almost print-like handwriting, Ammi had written,'Leaving you and the kids. Khudahafiz.'

Abbu turned the note over to see if there was something else there. Surely she couldn't write just one line and leave.

I felt something tighten inside me when I read that note. It solidified when Abbu's expression changed from worry to disbelief and then anger. It hardened when Abbu roared, looking up to the ceiling as if for some explanation. Now, nearly five months later, it hasn't loosened even one bit. If anything, I can feel more layers around it, protecting it, preventing it from breaking down.

We had all these career guidance classes in school just before the board exams a few months ago, and everyone was talking about their ambitions and what they wanted to do. Smriti, my best friend, kept quiet, just like me, because she knew that I wasn't going to say anything to the class. I'd told her already about what I wanted to do.

'But why?' she had asked.

'Why not? Why shouldn't I?' I asked her angrily. It only strengthened my resolve.

She shrugged and then, to my surprise, she clasped my hand and held it tightly.

'Fine. I'm with you, Maria,' she said.

I felt all choked up and my left eye was twitching furiously the way it did when I was trying to stop myself from crying. It made me look clownish and anyone who saw me trying to control my tears almost always burst out laughing.

Smriti didn't. She knew it was no laughing matter. Come what may, I was going to find my mother.

I found it really hard to believe that my mother would voluntarily leave us a couple of months before my tenth-standard board exams. I mean, how crazy was that? Teeth chattering from the cold on early mornings, we would sit down together and work out maths and read literature and she would explain physics to me. We'd drink warm Horlicks and watch the light steal over the sky in slow degrees and then she'd snap out of it first and ask me to focus on my books.

Without her guidance, there was no way I could do well in school. The teachers were baffled. From being one of their star students, I'd fallen right to the bottom of the class. It was clear I was going to do miserably in the board exams.

Read more by Andaleeb Wajid

Five years earlier, a friend's nasty comment makes Ananya start hating her body. She decides to change into a new person—one who effortlessly fits into all kinds of clothes, who shuns food unless it's salad, and who can never be called 'Miss Piggy'. She also cuts out everything from her 'old' life, including her best friend, Raghu, for being witness to her humiliation.

Ananya is on her way to becoming the Ananya of her dreams, but she's still a work in progress. One day, her parents announce that they're expecting a baby (at their age!). To make matters worse, Raghu reappears in her life . . .

Andaleeb Wajid's latest novel for young adults is a touching and funny story about a young girl's journey to acceptance and self-love.

Read the opening of *Mirror Mirror*

I thought my seventeenth birthday was going to be like any other. Boy, was I wrong.

My phone started beeping with birthday notifications from the moment it struck midnight, but I slept through it all. I even allowed myself to skip yoga in the morning and stay in bed for ten minutes longer than I usually did.

I glanced at my phone and saw that I had missed calls from my best friends, Nisha and Anirudh. We had holidays for Dasara in college, and had decided to meet at a cafe for lunch.

My parents had been subdued since morning. We had planned to go out for dinner, just the three of us. I should have known something was up when Papa agreed to my choice of the restaurant. He *hated* The Green Revolution. He insisted that grass is for cows and pooh-poohed my food choices all the time. But even that didn't tip me off.

During lunch with Nisha and Anirudh at the cafe, things were a bit weird and, at first, I couldn't figure out why. I observed the two of them and realized that they were not behaving as usual.

Anirudh looked troubled and Nisha seemed miserable. I suddenly realized what had happened. There was something going on between the two of them—something to do with their feelings for each other. Either Anirudh had said something to Nisha, or the other way around and it had made things awkward between them.

I tried and tried to get it out of them but they wouldn't tell me. They said that we'll talk the next day, after my birthday. I even blurted out what I was starting to suspect and going by Anirudh's blanched face, I knew I was on to something. Nisha just looked away, shaking her head.

The birthday just went downhill from there. I needed to speak to Nisha alone, but that made me feel guilty too.

Nisha and I had been friends since Class II and we had been inseparable. When Nisha opted for Kannada as her second language and I, Hindi, in Class V, I switched my second language and followed her right into her class, not worried about how I was going to study Kannada.

Then, Anirudh came along in Class VII. He was a typical bespectacled, shy boy who had a rather wicked sense of humour once you got to know him. He'd sprayed the back of our chemistry teacher's saree with ink once and all three of us got detention for that. Probably because we were sitting the closest to him and he looked much too innocent to do something of the sort on his own.

When we walked into the detention room, he was busy trying to capture a lizard using a plastic bag wrapped around his fist. I'd normally run miles away from such a person, but we somehow became good friends and we continued to be, right through our tenth and now in pre-university college.

A part of me was worried about what was going to happen after this. Anirudh was going to sit for competitive entrance exams and study to be a doctor, Nisha wanted to study architecture and I . . . I was still undecided.

I didn't really like the idea of them together. I'd be the third wheel, the 'kabab mein haddi' *all the time*. They'd want to meet up and spend time without me. And if we made plans to meet, they would either be waiting for me to come late or leave. Aaaargh.

Later that evening, as I dressed for dinner, I put the two of them firmly out of my mind and wore the new dress I'd bought for my birthday. I glanced at myself in the mirror quickly, bracing myself.

My arms were still chubby in spite of all the yoga, dieting and exercise. The churning in my stomach began as I wondered if I should wear some sort of a shrug to cover them up. Why did I think I could carry off a sleeveless dress? I'd need to diet for another ten years to have the kind of thin arms that I could show off.

I paced my room for a few minutes, itching to chew my fingernails. I could do it, I told myself sternly.

I could step out of this room and face the world with my chubby arms.

Thick ankles.
Round shoulders.
Ms Piggy.
Fat Ananya.

No, I couldn't.

I yanked the door of my wardrobe open and rummaged through my things. I found a white scarf, draped it around myself and walked out. The whispers in my head hadn't died down but they were a little less sibilant. I tried to push them to a corner of my mind as I walked outside.

Ma gave me a look, but didn't say anything. I should have realized then that something strange was going on.

It was only when I was halfway through my boring orange and spinach salad that I noticed that Papa fidgeting way too much. Ma kept looking at him uneasily. What was going on? I put my fork down, finally, and dabbed the corner of my lips with a napkin.

'What's the matter?' I asked.

Ma and Papa started and looked at each other once again. I had a terrible sort of premonition. Something was seriously wrong. Was one of them sick or dying or . . .

Ma mumbled something and my eyes widened. I must have misheard . . .